Cremir
l
Jesu

MW01062174

THE
DREAM
ASSEMBLY

Tales of Rabbi Zalman Schachter-Shalomi

Collected & Retold by Howard Schwartz
Illustrated by Yitzhak Greenfield

GATEWAYS / IDHHB, INC.
PUBLISHERS

Acknowledgements

Some of these tales have previously appeared in *Agada, Conservative Judaism, Four Worlds Journal, New Menorah Journal, New Traditions,* and *The Saint Louis Jewish Light.*
"The Torah of the Menorah" was co-authored by Zalman Schachter-Shalomi and Yonassan Gershom.

First Gateways Printing
Published by: Gateways/IDHHB, Inc.
PO Box 370, Nevada City, CA 95959, (916) 477-1116.

This book was originally published by Amity House, Inc., in 1988.

Library of Congress Cataloging-in-Publication Data

Schwartz, Howard, 1945-
    The dream assembly : tales of Rabbi Zalman Schachter-Shalomi / collected and retold by Howard Schwartz ; illustrated by Yitzhak Greenfield.
        p.   cm.
    ISBN: 0-89556-059-3 : $12.50
    1. Parables, Hasidic. 2. Hasidim- -Legends. 3. Schachter-Shalomi, Zalman, 1924- --Legends.   I. Schachter-Shalomi, Zalman, 1924- II. Title.
BM532.S373 1989
296.1'9- -dc20   89-23500
                                                                CIP

CONTENTS

In Memory of Our Teachers
Rabbi Aryeh Kaplan
and Rabbi Mordecai M. Kaplan

He who recites the words of the departed causes their lips to move in the grave. If this is so, how much more so do the soul's lips move when their teachings are recited? Imagine, then, the dialogue between Hillel and Shammai, both of which are the words of the living God, in the World of Truth that continues as long as their teachings are still recited by us here below.

Yishmru Da'at

THE SCRIBE'S PREFACE

It is said that the souls of the sages and rebbes are drawn from the Tree of Souls that grows in Paradise, behind the *Pargod*. The soul of Abraham was the first to descend from there, and the souls of our Fathers Isaac and Jacob followed suit. In this way the Holy One, blessed be He, makes certain that a soul from that Tree appropriate for each generation descends into this world. And from the first the Holy One noted which soul was intended for which generation, and this was a matter of great difficulty for him, as difficult as parting the waters of the Red Sea. For what could be more difficult than selecting the right soul to take its place among men at the right time?

And among the souls of that holy Tree was the soul of Reb Zalman. (There are those who say, God forbid, that it was the last soul selected to descend from that tree.) For from the very time of the Creation, the Holy One, blessed be He, had saved the soul of Reb Zalman for this time of upheaval and confusion. For that soul had the great strength to retain its clarity even in such a time when rebbes have begun to disappear from the earth and their memory is only to be found in books.

As all those who have met Reb Zalman can testify, the living spirit has manifested itself in him as it has in few others. Indeed, he need but reach up to the worlds above to pluck the teachings and tales he shares among us, and his spirit is able to ascend to that high place because it was there that his soul made its home for so long. And that is why his teachings resound with echoes from on high, for that indeed was their source.

As for the tales inscribed here, it is impossible for the humble scribe to know how true he has been to the words transmitted from above to below. For while some scribes listen with their ears, it is my blessing or my curse to hear only with my heart, as our sages said, "Words that issue from the heart enter the heart." And while the heart can recall in full the essence of what was heard better than any ear, the precise words have long since fallen away, and all that I had to go on was the deep imprint of the heart. This alone, then, has guided me in writing these tales down. And for this reason their failings must be counted my own, while their strengths are those of the Rebbe, who related them as he heard them on high. The poor scribe was merely able to hear them as they were echoed below and, as all wise men know, the distance between above and below is far too great to be bridged by mere words.

Let the reader of these tales then ignore the outer garment of the words and seek out their heart, for in seeking that heart he will arrive at the essence of the Rebbe's teachings, the seeds of which are sown herein. For perhaps the first truth that Reb Zalman learned was that in order to hear the whispers of the angels it is necessary to listen with the heart. This, then, is how these tales were first told, and this is how the humble scribe has sought to retell them. For it is their essence, above all, that matters, and it is in that essence, and that alone, wherein the truth that lies at the core of these tales can be found. May these chants and woven songs be accepted within the shadow of Thy hand. Amen and amen.

Reb Hayim Elya

BLESSING THE MOON

For a long time Reb Zalman had been working only in the sun and hadn't any moonlight. And every time he awoke at midnight to pray, the sky was cloudy and the moon was not to be seen. And before long the absence of moonlight from his life began to take its toll, and it was as if he were toiling in a barren vineyard where, despite all his efforts, nothing grew, for the plants required not only the sunlight, but the light of the moon as well.

So too was Reb Zalman deprived of the *mitzvah* of blessing the moon in its second quarter, when it is waxing. For every time he sought out the first disk of the new moon, it was hidden, and the blessing can only be made in the presence of the moon. And the absence of the moon from his life began to worry Reb Zalman, for the moon is the symbol of Israel's redemption. Just as the moon emerges from its exile, so too will Israel be brought back to the land of its fathers. And as long as the moon remained hidden from him, Reb Zalman remained in exile.

As time passed, Reb Zalman's longing for the moon increased, until it happened that he dreamed that he was standing in a vineyard at night. And the grapes in that vineyard were ripe on the vines, and the light of the new moon illumined them with a glow that seemed like it was coming from within. And in the dream Reb Zalman went from cluster to cluster, from leaf to leaf, saying *"Shalom Aleichem,"* and the clusters of grapes replied *"Aleichem Shalom."* Then Reb Zalman looked up and saw the moon in the sky, and at last it was fully revealed to him and not hidden behind the clouds. And the moon was so clear that it seemed to him that it was within his reach, and feeling suddenly confident, Reb Zalman jumped up toward the moon, and to his amazement he found himself rising upward towards the heavens, and he almost reached the moon. Then he descended slowly, and it was such a restful flight that Reb Zalman leaped up again, and once more he almost reached the moon. Then, the third time he leaped, Reb Zalman soared into the heavens all the way to the moon. And at the moment he touched it, Reb Zalman pronounced the blessing of the moon, which he had not said in so long. Then he drifted back down to the earth, and by the time he landed he felt that he had been fully restored and no longer suffered from an absence of moonlight.

That day, after he awoke, Reb Zalman convened a *Beit Din* and asked them the question: "Can one fulfill the obligation of blessing the moon in a dream?" Then the *Beit Din* debated this matter a long time, but at last they decided that it could indeed be done, since we learn in the *Tanach* that dreams reveal the truth, as in the dream of Jacob in which he saw the ladder reaching from earth into heaven, with angels ascending and descending upon it.

And that night, after the *Beit Din* had announced its decision, Reb Zalman had a vision in a dream in which he saw with his own eyes the ladder reaching from earth into heaven, and saw as well the angels ascending and descending its rungs. And in that moment of sudden illumination he discovered the true purpose of the angels—for they were bearing with them the prayers offered by those asleep, which the Holy One recognized as fully as those offered while awake, and accepted as completely. And he saw as well how those prayers were delivered to the angel Sandalphon on high and woven into a garland of prayers for the Holy One, blessed be He, to wear on his Throne of Glory. And after that Reb Zalman found that he made as many blessings in his dreams as he did while awake, for in a dream a man may unburden his soul as fully as when he is awake, and in the eyes of the Lord the one is as precious as the other.

THE DREAM ASSEMBLY

One day, when Reb Hayim Elya entered the *Beit Midrash,* he overheard a heated argument among Reb Zalman's Hasidim. The question was: what was the true purpose of *davening?* Reb Shmuel Leib said: "The purpose of *davening* is to recognize our Oneness with God." Reb Feivel the Light said: "The purpose of prayer is to attune body and soul." Reb Feivel the Dark said: "The purpose of *davening* is to open up the heart and let the heart sing its praises to God." Reb Sholem said: "It seems to me that you have overlooked the most basic purpose of prayer, which is to become a servant to God. And if you can't be a servant first, you don't have the right to be a teacher or a lover or anything else." Then Reb Hayim Elya spoke up and said: "It is stated in the *Siddur* that the whole purpose of *davening* is to bring down blessings. For without bringing down these blessings the prayer serves no purpose." Then Reb Aharon joined the discussion and said: "The purpose of *davening* is to perform *teshuvah,* for without *teshuvah,* what is the point of prayer?"

All at once the Hasidim grew silent, for each one had spoken, but Reb Zalman had said nothing, and all of them knew that he understood prayer better than anyone else. Therefore they waited for him to select the one who had best recognized its purpose, as if he were the judge in a *Beit Din*. But Reb Zalman did not address himself to the issue at all; instead he said: "I would like all of you to join me in a dream tonight." And at that he signaled for the evening prayers to begin, and said no more about it.

Now the Hasidim were quite confused about Reb Zalman's statement, for how is it possible to join another in a dream? Then Reb Shmuel Leib turned to the others and whispered: "I have read reports of such a thing—when the rabbis joined together in a dream assembly. But that was long ago, and no such assembly has been called in our time." And the others asked Shmuel Leib if he could recall any other details he had heard, such as how they could meet together. And he thought a long time and at last he said: "I recall that when we say the prayer upon retiring, and we come to the words 'Grant that we lie down in peace, O Lord,' we must lie down; and when we come to the words 'And assist me with Thy good counsel,' we must put our heads on the pillow and listen; and when we come to the words 'Guard our going out and our coming in,' we must close our eyes. And if each of these is done at the proper time, when the *Shekhinah* removes her veil, those who joined in prayer together will be joined together in a dream."

The Hasidim listened to these words, and just then Reb Zalman began to chant the first prayer. And that night each and every one of Reb Zalman's Hasidim lay down, put their heads on the pillow, and closed their eyes just as the *Shekhinah* turned to face herself in the mirror, and that night they met each other in a dream.

In the dream they found themselves in an orchard, which none of them had ever seen before. Everything about that orchard was strange. The fruit of the trees was un- familiar, consisting of unusual shapes, more like jewels than fruit. So too was the light of that orchard unusual, for it was illumined as if by the light of an unseen sun. And in the light they found they could see a great distance, almost from one

end of the world to the other. The Hasidim were very confused to find themselves there, but then Reb Shmuel Leib
remembered that Reb Zalman had told them to assemble
together in a dream, and he realized that they must be dreaming. But he said nothing about it to the others, out of the fear
that if they knew they were dreaming they might wake up.
Instead he merely said to them: "Have you forgotten? Reb
Zalman asked us to meet him here." And then the others did
recall that Reb Zalman had told them to assemble, but they
did not remember that the place of the meeting was a dream.
And since they knew they were supposed to be there, their
fears withdrew, and they looked around, to see if Reb Zalman
could be seen.

That is when they saw him—he was sitting beneath a
tree in a corner of the orchard, and all of the Hasidim hurried
to him and silently assembled in a circle around him. When
they had all been seated, Reb Zalman looked up. And the
Hasidim all noticed that although there was no doubt that it
was Reb Zalman they were with, still he seemed different. He
seemed younger and less burdened by the weight of the
world. And there was a wonderful smile on his face.

Then Reb Zalman said: "To bring us here together was
not a simple matter, far more difficult than finding a ladder
reaching from earth to heaven and ascending it. But now that
we are here, there is something of great importance that we
must accomplish. Know that there is a great mystery concerning the manner in which it is possible for prayers to ascend
to heaven. It also is no simple matter. The prayers themselves
do not have wings. They have to be carried into the heights.
And how are they carried? On the wings of a dove, as it is
written, *And he sent forth a dove.* But what is not known is that
each generation requires its own dove that can carry its
prayers into the hands of Sandalphon, the angel who weaves
those prayers into garlands of prayer that the Holy One,
blessed be He, wears on his Throne of Glory.

"Know that in every age this dove must be created anew.
The first dove was created by Abraham, single-handed. But
except for Moses there was no other who created the dove by

himself until the time of the Baal Shem Tov. Even the Ari required the assistance of Hayim Vital in order to bring the dove into being. In our own age there is no one who can bring this dove into being by himself. And therefore the creation of the dove is much more difficult. Great harmony is required, and an effort that must be perfectly shared. This, then, is why I have called upon us to assemble here: to bring the prayer dove into being, so that our prayers may also ascend in our own generation."

And then Reb Zalman stood up, and the Hasidim saw a look in his eyes that they had never seen before, a determination so complete that merely to gaze upon him was to be caught up in that power and to have no desire other than to share in undertaking that difficult, nay, impossible task.

Then Reb Zalman looked at Feivel the Dark and said: "You, Feivel, must create the feet of the bird, so that it can perch securely on any branch." And he turned to Feivel the Light and said: "And you, Feivel, must create its wings, so that it can soar into the heights of *Arabot*, the highest heaven." Then Reb Zalman turned to Reb Sholem and said: "You, Sholem, must create the body, and it must be perfect in every respect so that it can balance not only in the world of men, but in the Other World as well." Then Reb Zalman looked at Reb Hayim Elya and said: "You, Hayim Elya, must create its beak. This is the smallest part, but it is the most important. For the dove must transmit our prayers with its beak, and if the beak is imperfect in any way, the prayers will slip from its grasp and be lost." At last Reb Zalman turned to Reb Shmuel Leib and said: "And you, Shmuel Leib, must create its heart. For it is the heart that provides the *kavanah* without which the prayer has no more meaning than a body without breath."

Then, after speaking, Reb Zalman sat down beneath the tree and closed his eyes. And just before waking, the last thing each of them recalled was hearing the song of a dove, and that song was so full and so ripe and so sacred that the memory of it haunted every one of them for the rest of their lives. For each time they would open the *siddur* to pray they would hear the echo of the dove. And with its song echoing in their ears they knew, without doubt, that their prayers were destined to ascend into the heights.

THE NIGUN OF THE BIRDS

for Shira Schwartz

It was almost *Tu-bishvat*, the New Year for Trees, when the blessing of the *Sheheheyanu* is said over a fruit tasted for the first time that year. In Zholkiev it was the middle of a bitter winter, and not a fruit was to be found that he had not already tasted. For this reason Reb Zalman's spirits were low, for he had nothing with which to make the blessing. And it was his concern to see that no blessing was ignored.

That year *Shabbas Shirah* came one day before *Tu-bishvat*, and Reb Zalman still did not know where to find a first fruit. He carried his distress with him as he went outside to feed *kasha* to the birds on the eve of *Shabbas Shirah*. He went around to the places where the birds congregated, and spread *kasha* on the ground for them, for this was a *minhag* he always followed at that time of year.

Around noon that day Reb Hayim Elya arrived at Reb Zalman's house, and found him feeding the birds with tears in his eyes. Hayim Elya asked him what was wrong, and Reb Zalman told him that it appeared there would be no new fruit to bless that year. And as is the beginning, so will be the end. Hayim Elya wanted to divert Reb Zalman from this sadness,

so he asked him why he was feeding *kasha* to the birds. Reb
Zalman replied: "It was the birds who reminded the Children
of Israel of their joy in the crossing at the Red Sea, for they
flocked above them, singing. This inspired the people to
break out in the singing of the Song of the Sea. Therefore we
traditionally thank the birds on this day." Hayim Elya accepted the logic of this at once, but he was still curious to
know why it was *kasha* he was feeding them. Reb Zalman
replied: "Remember that the word *kasha* means a question.
Our question is: Where are we going to find a fruit, over
which to make the *Sheheheyanu?*" And Hayim Elya asked:
"But is *kasha* the traditional food?" And Reb Zalman replied:
"Only when we cannot find a new fruit."

Then Reb Zalman went on feeding the birds, singing the
Nigun of the Song of the Sea to himself. The birds, who had
been starving, were as happy to see the *kasha* as were the
Israelites to receive Manna from heaven. And after they had
fed themselves, some of the birds began to repeat the *nigun*.
At first Reb Zalman and Hayim Elya thought they were
imagining that the birds were singing that song, but in truth
it had happened, and they were both astonished. Hayim Elya
turned to Reb Zalman at once and said: "This singing of the
very same *nigun* by the birds is itself a miracle and a sign. And
the sign is that you must not give up hope that the first fruit
will arrive. For in this way the birds have replied to your
question." And when Reb Zalman heard this, his eyes grew
bright again, and a smile returned to his face. And it was
apparent to all that he had not given up hope.

All that day Reb Zalman hummed the *Nigun* of the Sea
to himself, and that night he slept peacefully, while his sleep
up till then had been fitful. And when he awoke the next
morning, when it was *Shabbas Shirah*, he felt as if his soul had
just returned from a long journey, as if he himself had crossed
the parted waters of the Red Sea.

That morning, when Reb Zalman opened the door and
looked outside, he saw a dove flying from afar, and he
thought to himself, "Why is it that the voice of the dove is so
sad? Is it not as the sages say because the *Shekhinah* mourns

with a sigh? But when the Messiah comes then will our tongue be full of song. So too, then, when the *Shekhinah* will no longer mourn, will the dove sing more sweetly than the nightingale." Just then the dove landed on a branch of a nearby tree, and that is when Reb Zalman saw that it was golden, for the light of its feathers radiated in the sun. And in its beak was an olive branch! Now Reb Zalman could not believe his eyes when he saw that dove and what it carried, for he knew that no such dove existed in this world, and that no olives grow in Poland in the winter, and that the golden dove must have brought them from very far. And suddenly Reb Zalman knew that the birds had heard his plea, and that the Holy One, blessed be He, had replied to his prayer.

And Reb Zalman walked beneath the branch of the tree in which the dove perched. And when he was standing directly beneath it, the dove dropped the olive branch into his hands. And as he caught it, Reb Zalman looked up at that bird, and he wondered if it might be the very dove of the Messiah, for what other could fly so far in such a short time? Just then the dove began to sing. And when Reb Zalman heard that song from the throat of the dove he was certain. For the song of that dove was none other than the *Nigun* of the Sea. And when he heard it, he heard it as if for the first time, and he knew without doubt that it was indeed that melody of the Children of Israel at the Sea. For in the voice of the dove he heard the voices of the Children singing in unison, with even the babes still in the wombs joining in.

Now Reb Zalman was amazed to see that golden dove and to hear its song, for he had heard tell of that dove before. For that dove was said to have been hammered out by King Solomon, who bestowed eternal life on it by pronouncing God's secret Name. Solomon created that dove to sing in times of joy and in times of sorrow, for there is a time and a season for everything. And why did the Messiah permit the abundant spirit of that dove, which belongs to him, to be made manifest by Solomon? Because it is said that until his blessed coming—may it be in our time!—the world is ruled by the teachings of Moses. But after the coming of the Messiah it will be governed by the teachings of Solomon. As for Solomon, he came to love the song of the dove so much that he never let it out of his presence.

The golden dove was lost when the Temple was destroyed. Then, many generations later, the sage Rabbah bar bar-Hannah was traveling with a caravan. They rode until evening fell and then stopped to rest. Later, after they had resumed their journey, Rabbah suddenly realized that he had forgotten to say the blessing after meals. He did not think it appropriate to say those prayers at a distance from where he had eaten, so he decided to return to the previous station.

Now Rabbah was a master of the law, but there were several other sages in that caravan. And it occurred to him that not all of them would agree with this interpretation of the law. And since he did not want to debate the matter, since it would take him even further from that place, instead he told his companions that he was returning to the camp site in order to recover a golden dove that he had left behind. Naturally they wished him luck in finding it, for they recognized that such a treasure could not be abandoned.

So it was that Rabbah continued through the dark until at last he reached the previous site. There he uttered the prayers, and as he finished he looked down and saw an object buried in the sand that glittered in the moonlight. Rabbah went over and dug it out, and to his complete amazement he found that it was a golden dove. He took the dove in his hands, and as he held it, it seemed to quiver as if it were trying to flap its wings. Greatly surprised, Rabbah opened his hands, and the golden dove took flight.

The golden dove was also seen by the Ari, by Rabbi Adam, by the Maharal, and, in our time, by the Baal Shem Tov. This took place when the Baal Shem Tov was praying with his Hasidim and ascended the ladder of their prayers into the celestial realm. There he glimpsed the dove in the branches of a tree, and heard its wonderful song. He tried to ascend high enough to capture that golden bird and bring it back to this world, but just when it was within his reach the ladder collapsed, for his disciples, who had already finished praying, had lost patience and left the synagogue. Afterward the Baal Shem revealed what had happened, and told them that if he had indeed succeeded in bringing that dove to nest under his roof, peace would have come to the world at last.

The next to see the golden dove was Rabbi Nachman, who captured the miraculous dove by including it in one of his tales. For once Rabbi Nachman had included anything in one of his tales, he came to know it completely, and its whole history was revealed to him from the very beginning. Thus he learned that it was the golden dove of the Messiah, whose song awaits those of the righteous who take their place in the World to Come. But it was Reb Zalman to whom it was revealed who had sent the golden dove into the world, and why. For it was none other than the Messiah himself, to see if the world was ready for him to come. The golden dove was first sent forth shortly after the Fall, but of course the world was not ready. Since then the Messiah has sent the dove out once in every century to test the waters. Sometimes it is seen, but most often it remains invisible to the mortal eye, for its body is a spirit body, which only the eye of the spirit of another can see. And few are those among men who let the eyes of their souls lead them.

And as Reb Zalman stood beneath that tree, in which the golden dove uttered its song, he had a vision in which he stood before the palace of the Messiah known as the Bird's Nest, as if in its presence, and before the vision ended he saw that the Messiah stands ready to pass through the gates of heaven whenever the dove tells him that the world is ready.

So it was that Reb Zalman was able to say the *Sheheheyanu* over the first fruit that year, and to taste that sweet blessing as never before. And with the pits of those olives he planted three trees, in the hope that the dove might one day nest there. May it come to pass in our day and our time! Amen.

THE TALE OF THE TEFILLIN

One night Reb Zalman had a dream in which he was told to go to the town of Tismenitz. That was all he remembered when he awoke. And even though he did not know why he was supposed to go there, or who he was supposed to meet, Reb Zalman packed a few things and set out for Tismenitz, where he knew not a single soul.

It was almost evening when Reb Zalman arrived, and he first *davened* in his room and then finished unpacking. And it was then that he discovered, to his horror, that his *tefillin* were missing. Now Reb Zalman never forgot to bring his *tallis* and *tefillin,* no matter what else he might forget to bring. And he was so perturbed that he was ready to return to Zholkiev then and there. In the meantime a storm arose and a heavy rain began to fall. And when he thought the matter over, he realized that he could not get a wagon to travel that night, for it was too dangerous. And it was forbidden to bring oneself into danger in order to fulfill one of the *mitzvot.*

Then Reb Zalman considered if it would be possible to fulfill the *mitzvah* of *tefillin* in a purely spiritual sense, by seeking the unification through *kavanah,* without using actual *tefillin.* He debated this matter to himself, and he concluded that this is what he would do only if there were no other choice. But it was too soon to reach that conclusion, for Reb Zalman had not yet searched for *tefillin* in that town.

Then Reb Zalman left his room in the inn, and set out in the rain to look for a synagogue in that town where he might find *tefillin.* By asking those he met on the street, he was able to find his way to the town's only synagogue. He knocked on the door of the *Beit Knesset,* and it was opened by a Gentile who served as the caretaker there. When the caretaker saw that Reb Zalman was a Jew, he admitted him at once. Then Reb Zalman asked him if there were any extra *tefillin* to be found in that synagogue. At first the caretaker did not know what Reb Zalman was talking about, but after he described the *tefillin* and how they were applied, the caretaker became excited and told Reb Zalman that he had found a bag of *tefillin* just that evening, which had been concealed in a crevice behind one of the bookcases in the *Beit Midrash.* He went into the adjoining room of the House of Study, and came out with a bag of *tefillin,* which he handed to Reb Zalman. And when Reb Zalman opened that bag of *tefillin* and saw them and heard how they had just been found, he knew with a strange certainty that he had been sent to that town to recover those very *tefillin,* and all at once he became very calm and filled with an inner peace.

Then Reb Zalman examined those *tefillin,* which he recognized were very old, although they had been carefully preserved in that bag, made of the finest velvet. And he recognized as well that those *tefillin* had been made with the greatest care by one highly skilled in the making of *tefillin.* And he was filled with a longing to put those *tefillin* on then and there, but he restrained himself, for he wanted to savor their power at the morning prayers, when they are required to be worn.

Now Reb Zalman did not want to leave that synagogue without taking those *tefillin,* but he felt that it would not be enough to ask the caretaker for them, that he must have permission from the Gabbai. Just then Reb Zalman heard the sound of someone studying out loud in the *Beit Midrash*. He went through the doorway that separated the two rooms, and there he saw an old man studying the Talmud. Reb Zalman greeted the old man and asked him what tractate it was that he was studying, and the man told him that it was Haggigah. Now when Reb Zalman heard this, a shiver passed through his body, for he suddenly remembered the story of the man who had always studied Haggigah, that tractate alone, all of his days. Others had mocked him for this, but when he had died an old man had arrived at his funeral who was unknown to any of the others, and he had delivered a wonderful eulogy for the departed, in which he highly praised his decision to devote himself solely to that tractate. The story went on to say that soon afterwards that same man, who had passed away, came in a dream to three of those who had been present at his funeral. And to each of them he told the true identity of the old man who had spoken so highly of him at his funeral. For it was none other than the angel of Haggigah. And suddenly, as he looked upon that old man, it seemed to Reb Zalman that he had an other-worldly quality, and it seemed as if his face were surrounded by an aura.

Then, with fear and trembling, Reb Zalman asked the old man of such strange visage if he might be permitted to keep those *tefillin* which the caretaker had found in the *Beit Midrash* that night. And the old man looked up from the pages of Haggigah, and Reb Zalman saw that his eyes were illumined in a way unlike those of men. And the old man simply nodded, and turned back to the pages of the book. Then Reb Zalman thanked him, and seeing that the old man intended to say no more, he took his leave of him and that synagogue and returned to the inn.

There, once again, Reb Zalman had a strong urge to try on the *tefillin*, but again he resisted the temptation. And that night, in a dream, Reb Zalman again met the man of the strange visage. And the old man then revealed to him his true identity. For he himself had once made those *tefillin*, and he had also written the text of the parchment inside the box of the *tefillin*, for in his life he had been a *sopher*. And those *tefillin* had belonged to him while he was alive, but now he made his home in Paradise, among the righteous. As for the *tefillin*, he had used them every day until he had been taken prisoner during the war, and during all that time he was forbidden to possess *tefillin*. Therefore he had turned all of his *kavanah* to those *tefillin*, which rested in a drawer in his home in a faraway city. And he thought of them with great intensity especially during the morning prayers, which he said from memory every day. Miraculously, he was freed after the war and returned to his home and found those *tefillin* where he had left them, completely intact. Then he had treasured them for all the rest of his life, and before his death he had hidden them in that synagogue.

Then, in the dream, the soul of the old man revealed the secret of those *tefillin*, for before his death he had prayed for those *tefillin* to carry his blessing to the first one who prayed with them when they were found. Thus he had come back to his world to see who it was who would receive those *tefillin*, for it was destined that they be discovered that night. And he had been very happy to find that Reb Zalman was the one to receive them.

Now when Reb Zalman awoke from this dream, he saw that it was nearly dawn, and that the time had come to lay those *tefillin*. But he decided that he must not do it in that inn, but in the very synagogue where the old man had prayed and where they had been hidden for so long. Then Reb Zalman dressed as quickly as he could and took the bag of the *tefillin* and ran to that synagogue and arrived just as the sun was rising. And when he came inside, he saw to his amazement that nine old men had gathered there, and that he was the tenth. And those old men were delighted to see him, for now they had enough for a Minyan. And Reb Zalman lovingly put on those *tefillin*, and when he finished binding his hand and placing the box of the *tefillin* on his forehead, he suddenly felt surrounded by a glowing light, as if he were in the very presence of the *Shekhinah*. And at that moment he came to understand the most hidden and recondite reason for the *mitzvah* of the *tefillin*, a secret that only a handful of *Tzaddikim* had ever been privileged to discover, among them the Ari, the Maharal, the Baal Shem Tov and Rabbi Nachman of Bratslav.

After that, every time Reb Zalman bound the straps of that *tefillin* upon his hands and placed the box as a frontlet between his eyes, the mystery would reveal itself anew, and the world was illumined all over again.

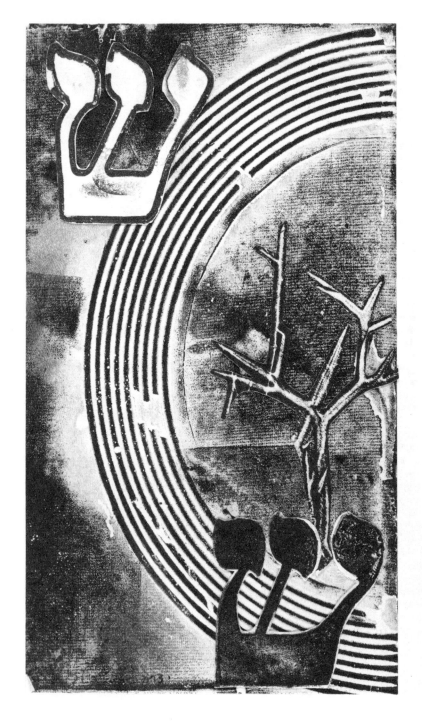

THE TALE OF THE COVENANT

For ten years Reb Hayim Elya of Buczacz had been writing the parchment strips for the box of the *tefillin* and the *Mezzuzah* and writing and repairing *Sefer Torahs*. And he wrote down every letter with care, making certain that there were not any extra letters, and also that no letter that was needed was missing. As required, he did not write even a single word of these texts from memory, and he pronounced every word before copying it from the correct text. He also took care that every letter had a space around it, and was so formed that it could easily be distinguished from similar letters. Above all, he wrote the words with *kavanah*, drawing them into himself and listening to their echo within as he wrote down each and every word.

In days gone by, Hayim Elya had learned the holy work of the *sopher* from Reb Yehuda, and he had studied Torah from Reb Zvi, whom he had also served as a scribe until Reb Zvi had departed to become a *Rosh Yeshivah* in Warsaw. From time to time Hayim Elya heard reports of Reb Zalman, and once a book of the teachings of rebbes that Reb Zalman had edited had come into his hands. It was there that Hayim Elya

had first read the teaching and tales of Reb Nachman of
Bratslav, who came to serve as a great inspiration for him.
And Hayim Elya also greatly admired Reb Nachman's scribe,
Reb Nussan, partly because his own father's name was also
Nussan, and because Reb Nussan had so faithfully preserved
the teachings of his Rebbe.

Once it happened that Hayim Elya had a dream in which
he found himself at a *d'var Torah* given by Reb Zalman. In the
dream Hayim Elya found himself writing down his words as
they were spoken, and barely had time to look up at the
Rebbe. But once, when Reb Zalman paused for a long time,
Hayim Elya was able to look around him, and he saw that
there were nine other Hasidim in that room, and that each
and every one of them was also writing down the Rebbe's
words. And Hayim Elya realized that all of them must also be
sophers, like himself, and he was amazed at this, for few were
those who took the path of the *sopher,* and he had never seen
so many gathered in one place.

Then, in the dream, Reb Zalman began to tell a tale, and
as Hayim Elya recorded it, he also listened intently and he
found to his amazement, that it was a story about himself. It
was the tale of how he had been initiated into the Law by the
loving care of his father, and of his background and love for
Reb Nachman, and it went on to reveal great mysteries and
secrets that only Hayim Elya could have known. And as he
wrote down those words, Hayim Elya was completely mystified, for he could not imagine how Reb Zalman could have
known these things. And then he woke up. And when he did,
Hayim Elya was inclined to regard this dream as a sign, for
he had been greatly moved by it. And therefore he decided to
seek out Reb Zalman in the town of Zholkiev.

When Hayim Elya reached the home of Reb Zalman, he
wrote a *qvittle,* in which he stated that he would like to meet
with him. And Hayim Elya took care even with the writing of
that *qvittle,* for such were the ways of scribes. The *qvittle* was
delivered to Reb Zalman along with those of several other
Hasidim. One by one the Hasidim were called in to speak to
Reb Zalman, while Hayim Elya waited. Finally, when he was

the only one left, he was called in. When at last he took a place in Reb Zalman's study, the Rebbe did not introduce himself, but said: "You are a *sopher.*" And Hayim Elya acknowledged that it was true. And Reb Zalman said: "A small addition to this house has just been completed which will serve as a room for solitude. It needs a *Mezzuzah.* I have a *Mezzuzah* that used to belong to a great *Tzaddik.* Alas, it fell into water and its letters were dissolved. I saved the parchment and now wish to have the text written anew. But I need special intention for the words 'One,' 'this day,' 'when thou sittest in thy house.' Would you be willing to write it for me?" And Hayim Elya gladly agreed to write the *parshiyot* for him.

Then Reb Zalman got up and gathered together the implements with which to write: the parchment, the quill and ink, as well as the ruler and the bone stylus for making the lines on the parchment. After that Hayim Elya studied the parchment, to be certain that it was without blemish. For the condition of the *Mezzuzah* is a reflection of the state of a man's life, and therefore it must be as perfect as possible. Hayim Elya was pleased with the parchment and he asked Reb Zalman for a Sopher's *Tikkun* for, although he knew the *Shema* by heart, he always wrote from that text rather than from memory. And with the *Tikkun* open in front of him he began to write the text on the side of the parchment nearer the flesh, as required. He took great care in forming each of the letters, while Reb Zalman watched. In fact, he wrote so slowly that it took him three hours, until it was nearly time for *Minhah.* Then he handed the parchment to Reb Zalman, who read it and saw that it was flawless. And Reb Zalman smiled a wonderful smile, and said: "The letters you have formed are almost as perfect as the words themselves. Tell me, would you be willing to serve as my scribe?" And Hayim Elya knew that it had been *beshert* because of his dream, and he agreed to serve at once.

After that Hayim Elya accompanied Reb Zalman to *Minhah,* and after the evening prayers Reb Zalman invited him to remain at his house that night. Then, the next morning, after *Shaharis,* Reb Zalman took Hayim Elya on a walk in the nearby forest, where he often came to meditate. He brought Hayim Elya to the very clearing that was his favorite place, in the center of which was a beautiful, ancient tree. The two Hasidim spoke as they walked, and soon found that they had made a full circuit around that tree. Then Reb Zalman said: "Perhaps it is here, in the presence of this tree, that we might make our covenant. For it is at this tree that sometimes I stand, sometimes I sit, sometimes I walk, and sometimes I root myself." And Hayim Elya agreed that it might be spoken there, and written down at a later time. As they walked, they spoke of friendship and the grace of God for having brought them together. And when they had returned to the place where they had started, Reb Zalman compared their covenant to a *ketubah,* a marriage contract. And he observed that the Torah itself is a *ketubah,* since it is a covenant between God and Israel. Then Reb Zalman said: "Since we have already made one circuit around this tree, let us make six more, each one of which will bind us closer." And he began to walk, and Hayim Elya walked with him, and they followed the round shadow that tree cast on the ground, for the sun stood above it in the sky. And he added: "But do our sages not say that there is no *ketubah* in which there isn't some quarrel?" And then Reb Zalman smiled wryly, and said: "In the parchment of the *Mezzuzah* you wrote for me, I saw that you favored the lettering of Reb Yitzhak Luria." Hayim Elya replied: "Yes, and that is because writing letters is like repairing broken vessels; each letter written is an act of *Tikkun* in itself. And the holy Ari was the one who revealed the teachings of the broken vessels and their *Tikkun.*"

Then Reb Zalman astonished Hayim Elya by saying: "Nevertheless, I want you to write using lettering of Reb Yosef Caro, for he was the author of the *Shulhan Aruch,* the Code of the Law we live by, and he also was an intimate of the angels. And there is no other I know of who was rooted so well in both worlds." Now Hayim Elya was silent for a long time, for he was quite certain that the style of lettering he had learned was the right one for himself, and also that he felt far closer to the *neshamah* of the Ari than to that of Reb Yosef Caro.

Yet he also knew that in becoming Reb Zalman's *sopher* he must be prepared to learn to work in a new way. And when he had finally resolved this matter for himself, he said: "In those cases where it seems that the script of Yosef Caro is appropriate, I will be willing to write it, but in those cases where it seems that only the script of the Ari will serve, then I will insist on using that one." And Reb Zalman smiled when he heard these words, which came at the end of the second circuit. And as they started upon the third circuit Reb Zalman said: "Let us now put all matters of quarrel behind us. For I fully accept that once you pick up the pen, you must write as you see fit. Just remember this: it is my light that you are going to be creating a vessel for. See to it that it holds the light and does not shatter."

After this both Reb Zalman and Hayim Elya were breathing lighter, and they were happier as well, for Reb Zalman had given Hayim Elya the freedom he needed, and Reb Zalman felt assured that the vessel would not break and his light be scattered and lost. Now, with these assurances, they began the fourth circuit. Here Reb Zalman spoke of the Written Law and the Oral Law. And Reb Zalman said: "Here is a secret: Moshe received the Written Law during the day and the Oral Law at night; thus God revealed the Torah to him during the day, and explained it at night. And those souls that were conceived on the sixth day during the day have souls of the Written Law. But those who were conceived that night have souls linked to the Oral Law. Now, I know that my soul comes from the Oral side, while yours is one of those attached to the Written Law. That is why I need you to translate what I say." And Hayim Elya understood much more clearly how he could serve Reb Zalman, and he counted himself among the fortunate.

On the fifth circuit Reb Zalman recounted how the rabbis told of those who, unable to study the five Books of Moses, could at least recite the five Books of the Psalms. And they believed that it was counted in the eyes of the Holy One, blessed be He, as if they had studied the five Books of Moses. Then Reb Zalman said: "Let us then invoke the spirit of King

David, author of the Psalms, and pray that anyone involved with these tales should have the reading of them accounted to him, as if he had studied the Torah." And Hayim Elya joined Reb Zalman in making that prayer, for he too devoutly wished that it be true.

At the turning of the sixth circuit, Reb Zalman said: "Each turn around this tree we bind ourselves to the spiral of *gilgul*. And who knows if our wandering souls were matched once before in another life? Now each time a *neshamah* goes through the cycle of life, it is either purified or soiled. Let us promise to do everything in our power so that we may return our soul to our Maker even purer than when it was received." And they made a vow to this effect.

Now when Reb Zalman and Hayim Elya reached the seventh spiral, they found that they were calm and peaceful, and that there was really nothing else that needed to be said. So they walked around the seventh time in complete silence. For that spiral represented the Sabbath, the day of rest, on which all outstanding matters become resolved, and the world basks in the glow of the Divine Presence. And as they walked together around that final circuit, it seemed to Hayim Elya as if a sacred light had been sown in their presence, and that a Tree of Light took root and sprouted there. And sheltered in that Tree of Light, Hayim Elya knew that their covenant had indeed been blessed.

A PURE VESSEL

for Elana

Now the *neshamah* of Reb Zalman of Zholkiev always knew when it was time to seek out the *neshamah* of Reb Hayim Elya, his scribe. At such times Hayim Elya might have two dreams about Reb Zalman on the same night, and discover in the morning that his wife, Tselya, had also had a dream in which Reb Zalman was present. Then Hayim Elya would know that the spirit of Reb Zalman was seeking him out, and that he had sent him three dreams that night, two of which he had received, and the third which had come to him through his wife. For she had an ability to receive dreams meant to reach Hayim Elya, which somehow failed to penetrate his sleep, and therefore turned to Tselya, who was a pure vessel.

Now in the spring of his thirty-sixth year, Hayim Elya had a series of dreams about Reb Zalman in a short period. In one of these dreams Hayim Elya found himself in Reb Zalman's home, visiting with his fifteen children—for in the dream Reb Zalman had six more children than he did in this world, where he had fathered nine. Also, in that dream, each child had a different mother, a strange fact which haunted

Hayim Elya when he awoke. Now when Hayim Elya had reported this dream to him, Reb Zalman said: "Surely there is a mystery here, Hayim Elya. For the truth is that my wife and I have a wish to have one last child, and for that child to be conceived in *Eretz Yisrael*, where we hope to be next year, so that we might fulfill the injunction of the *Seder:* 'Next year in Jerusalem.' Now that would be my tenth child. And consider that five of my children are married, and their husbands and wives have become my children as well, and the total comes to fifteen, as in your dream."

When Hayim Elya had heard this he said: "That is truly amazing, Rebbe, and augurs, I hope, that your wife will in fact conceive your tenth child in the Holy Land. But tell me, how do you account for the fact that in the dream each child had a different mother, for I cannot imagine what this might mean."

To this Reb Zalman replied: "Every human being serves as a vessel to many spirits. When one of these takes possession, it colors our soul and hovers in our presence. Now there are many spirits for whom I have served as a host, among them the spirits of the Ari, the Baal Shem, and Rabbi Nachman of Bratslav. And when I felt the sparks of their souls ignite in my being, I did everything in my power to be as pure a vessel as possible, to permit them full expression. For I have always longed to be a rock through which the waters of life would run.

"Now, as it is with a man, so too is it with his wife. For in the course of her life a woman may open herself to many spirits, for a woman who is a pure vessel may receive many sacred sparks. After all, what is a child but a spark of life that has taken root? And when a *Tzaddik* comes to unite with his wife, whom he loves like his own flesh, he also intends to unite with the *Shekhinah,* who serves as the spiritual mother to any child conceived during the time she is present. And every second the *Shekhinah* has a new face. That is why every one of my children had a different mother in your dream."

Hayim Elya was filled with joy at these words, which so illuminated the mystery. But when he turned back to Reb

Zalman he saw that his spirits seemed to have fallen, as if some kind of change had taken place. And he said: "What is it, Rebbe. Why are you suddenly so crestfallen?" And Reb Zalman replied: "I too have recently had a dream which has been haunting me. And strange to say, this dream was very much like a dream of Reb Nachman's, one I am certain that you know of. In that dream Reb Nachman was handed a book, and when he took it he did not know how to hold it, and when he opened it, it seemed completely strange to him, a foreign language in a foreign script. And Reb Nachman grieved, for he longed to know the meaning of the message.

"Now in my dream I found myself in the *Beit Knesset*, the House of Prayer. And with me were all my opponents, those who feel my approach is too severe, and those who feel that my methods are not severe enough. In the dream all of these had gathered there that I might reveal to them a secret about how to *daven*. For they had agreed to ignore all my faults for that one day, that I might transmit this secret to them. And I approached the pulpit and opened the *siddur* and began to pray, but all at once I discovered that I could no longer read the words, nor did I recall the melodies of any of the prayers. Then, out of desperation, I began to chant 'Oy, oy, oy, oy.' And I was afraid to turn around, that all of them might know that I knew nothing."

Hayim Elya marveled at how Reb Zalman's dream so closely resembled Reb Nachman's, and how both dreams revealed how far their spirits had fallen. For like Reb Nachman, Reb Zalman continually sought to ascend the Tree of Light, and if he failed to reach a rung, he was compelled to start over from the bottom. That is how it is for those who continually seek out their celestial soul. But never did this falling back cause Reb Zalman to despair, for he understood that there is no greater blessing than to begin again.

That same night Hayim Elya was blessed with an abundant dream which had surely been sent for Reb Zalman. For just as his wife had received a dream intended for him, so too did Hayim Elya sometimes receive a dream intended for his Rebbe, and what is finer than to serve as a vessel, whose

blessing it is to receive and transmit? So too did Moshe receive
the Oral and the Written law that was revealed to him in one
long breath, one kiss of the *Shekhinah,* and so too does a rebbe
serve as a vessel for the Holy One, blessed be He.

Now in this dream great strife afflicted the world, and
everywhere were to be found the destroyers of books, who
sought to turn every book into kindling until the sacred texts
were no longer to be found. Even the Torah had been burned
so many times that the heavens were filled with the flying
letters of a multitude of scrolls, and rare indeed was anyone
who recalled its truth. In that time Reb Zalman was one of the
last who knew its teachings, both in word and in spirit, and
he was also one of the few who knew where the remaining
scroll had been hidden until the time of darkness had passed.
And in the dream Reb Zalman took several Hasidim with him,
among them Reb Aharon, Reb Simcha and Hayim Elya, and
brought them to the cave where the scroll of the last Torah
had been concealed.

Now when they entered that cave, all of the Hasidim
immediately fell asleep. And they slept for long stretches, and
when they woke up they did not realize that they had been
asleep. For such was the spell that the sleepers remained
ignorant of how much time had been lost. Only Reb Zalman
sought to remain awake in that place, and even when he
succumbed to sleep, he at least remembered that he had been
sleeping when he woke up. And while he was awake Reb
Zalman sought to discover how the spell might be broken, so
that the Word of God might make its way into the world once
more. And in this way he discovered at the end of one passage
in the cave a basket of apples from the Tree of Life. And that
passage had been closed off for many years and was filled
with the scent of those apples, which had remained as fresh
as if they had just been picked. And when he breathed in that
wonderful fragrance, Reb Zalman became fully awake, and
remembered all that he had forgotten, and understood what
must be done so that the others might also be awakened from
their long sleep. Then he picked up the basket and sought to
carry it outside of the cave, but the instant he carried it beyond

the threshold the apples withered, and the scent they gave off was repugnant. Then Reb Zalman quickly carried the basket back into the cave, where the apples were restored at once. It was then that Reb Zalman understood that nothing more could be accomplished until he learned the secret of how to take the apples out of that place without causing them to wither. And in the dream he discovered this secret, and in the end he carried out the apples and brought their sweet scent first to his Hasidim, and then to the rest of the world, and all who shared in their fragrance were awakened to the truth. But how he did this Hayim Elya could not remember when he woke up, much to his chagrin.

That morning Hayim Elya hurried to tell Reb Zalman this dream. And Reb Zalman was deeply moved to hear it, and afterwards he said: "This dream, Hayim Elya, is the other half of the dream I had, and they fit together into a whole like day and night, each one shedding the light of understanding on the other. There can be no doubt but that this dream was sent to me through you, for somehow the gates of sleep must have been locked, and would not admit Duma, the Prince of Dreams, to deliver this message directly to me. And you, Hayim Elya, are surely a pure vessel to have received this dream, illumined from within by sparks that once fell from shattered vessels, which can now be restored.

"Ah, but how I wish, Hayim Elya, that you had not forgotten how I succeeded in carrying the apples out of that cave without causing them to wither. Now I will have to discover it all over again!"

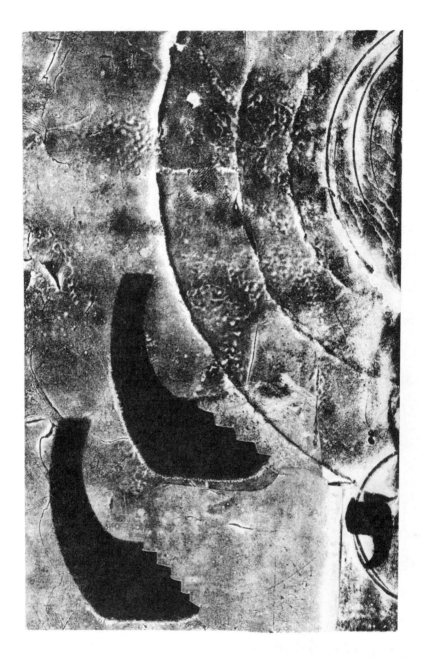

THE TALE OF THE SHOFAR

for Paul Horn

*As in the material world sound travels great distances
from place to place, so that two places that are remote
from one another are bound and connected only by sound,
so in the spiritual realm it is possible
to transcend space and rise above it.*

Rabbi Nachman of Bratslav,
Likkute Etzot Hadash

N ow Reb Zalman and Reb Hayim Elya both had
shofars which had come from the same ram. They
had found that ram caught in a thicket as they had walked
together one *Erev Yom Kippur,* early in the morning, and they
had performed the ritual of *kapparot* upon it, and then shared
the horns, which were both the same length and each of
which served as a fine shofar. And before long they discovered that when one shofar was blown, the other would
reverberate, and the echo of a faint blast would be emitted
from it. And they also discovered that if both shofars were

blown on at the same time, those in the presence of one would insist they had heard two shofars, although only the one was to be seen.

One year it happened that Reb Zalman departed for the forest outside Zholkiev with a few of his Hasidim, to spend the period from *Rosh Hashanah* to *Yom Kippur* with only a canopy of stars between him and his Creator, as the Baal Shem had often chosen to do on the Days of Awe. So it was that shortly after his arrival in the forest, on the day before *Erev Rosh Hashanah*, Reb Zalman walked off alone and made his way through the dense woods until he discovered a clearing deep in the forest, which had been formed by a circle of seven of the oldest and tallest trees. He first walked clockwise around that circle, for that is the direction of ascent, as with the sun, and with each circle he completed he felt as if he had ascended a rung of Jacob's Ladder, and he knew that he had reached a sacred place. He intended to circle there seven times, but the haunting song of a nearby bird confused him, so that he was not certain if he had circled seven times or eight. Then Reb Zalman sat down in the center of the circle, but as soon as he did so, he felt as if he were falling. Yet it was not the kind of fall of one who loses his grip on a mountain, but the weightless fall of a leaf, as it drifts down from a high place to the world below. And that fall continued much longer than Reb Zalman would have thought possible, and at last he realized that he had no way of knowing how long that fall would last, or where it was that he was falling toward. All around him there was a swirl of colors like the shades of every color of autumn leaf, but he could not focus on any object, and the world continued to swirl around him. That is when Reb Zalman realized that he must have fallen into the Void of which Reb Nachman speaks in "The Torah of the Void," the edge of which is never further away than a single false step. And it was then that he recognized that he must have been mistaken in his counting, and circled eight times, instead of seven, for the seventh rung of Jacob's Ladder is that of the sage, on which he would have been safe. But the eighth rung is that of the Messiah, and to ascend to that place before the Messiah has come is fraught with danger.

It was then, falling in that place, that Reb Zalman found himself thinking strange thoughts. It entered his mind that this endless falling could be all that truly exists, and that it might well exist only in his own mind. In that case the world he had known would never have existed except as *Olam Hatohu*, the World of Chaos, and thus merely as an illusion. Or, even worse, it might have been *'Alma d' Shikra*, a World of Lies. And who would be responsible for such a terrible deception if not the Creator he had come to that forest to seek out? But in the same instant that he found himself questioning the intentions of the Creator, Reb Zalman understood that he had fallen prey to temptation in that place. And then his mind grew clear, and he recognized that he must find a way out of that dilemma. It was then that he remembered that all he had carried with him was his shofar, which had hung from his shoulder, and now floated with him in that place. And he reached out and took hold of the shofar, and blew a long blast on it, that echoed for a few seconds, and then was replaced by the silence that had reigned in the first place. Nor had he stopped falling, as he had hoped. To his dismay he was as alone in that place as when he had first begun to fall.

Now, at the same time, several hundred miles away, in the town of Buczacz, Reb Hayim Elya was working in the *Beit Midrash*, trying to complete the writing of a *Sefer Torah* before *Simhat Torah*, when it was to be read for the Bridegroom of the Beginning. For Hayim Elya had been commissioned to write that *Sefer Torah* by the *Hevra Kadishah* of Reb Zalman's town of Zholkiev, and Reb Zalman would be the first to be called to read from it. All at once Hayim Elya heard a strange sound, like a faint blast blown on a shofar, coming from the *Aron Hakodesh* in the *Beit Knesset* next to the House of Study where he was working. And Hayim Elya recognized that sound at once, for it was the sound his shofar made whenever Reb Zalman would blow on his shofar, no matter how far away he might have been. And when he heard that sound, Hayim Elya understood that somewhere Reb Zalman was calling to him, for the shofars saw to it that their fates were tied together like the two ends of a long thread. Nor was that thread in any danger of breaking as long as they retained possession of those shofars.

But then it occurred to Hayim Elya that it was a strange time for Reb Zalman to blow a blast on the shofar, for it was his practice not to blow on it for one day before it was taken out on *Rosh Hashanah*. And then Hayim Elya understood that something must be wrong, for otherwise Reb Zalman would never have blown on the shofar at that time. Then he looked down at the *Sefer Torah* he was writing, and he saw that the last lines he had written were *Even if you are an outcast at the ends of the heavens, from there the Lord your God will gather you, from there He will fetch you.* This confirmed all of his fears; and then, without hesitation, Hayim Elya reached into the *Aron Hakodesh* where the shofar was stored, and took it out, and felt it still reverberating from the blast of its brother. Then he lifted up the shofar and drew in a deep breath and blew a long blast on it, that was snatched up by the wind and carried heavenward on the wings of a white bird that was passing at that instant. And far away, in the Void where he was still falling, Reb Zalman felt his shofar suddenly begin to vibrate, and then it gave forth a ghostly blast, in which Reb Zalman recognized the voice of Hayim Elya. And he realized that the bond between them was still unbroken, and that the world must therefore exist. And no sooner did he understand this than the swirl around him began to slow and stop. Soon he was able to see the world in focus, and to feel the warmth of the sun as it filled the clearing where he sat, in the middle of the circle, with the shofar still reverberating in his hand.

A TZADDIK IN
SEARCH OF A SCRIPT

for Esperanza

R eb Zalman called Reb Shmuel Leib and Feivel the Dark and Feivel the Light and asked them to form a *Beit Din,* a court of law. Reb Sholem and Reb Hayim Elya were to serve as the scribes of the court.

Here, then, were the proceedings, as Reb Hayim Elya recalled them: Reb Zalman sighed with a heavy heart and said that he wished the *Beit Din* to meet after the morning prayer to hear a dream of his, and to perform the ritual of *Hatavat Halom,* in which a dream is interpreted.

Once the *Beit Din* had been constituted, Reb Zalman stood before them, and Shmuel Leib, speaking for the court, said: "All interpretations are of God. Please tell us your dream." Then Reb Zalman said three times: "I saw a dream, may it be for good." And Shmuel Leib replied: "The dream you have seen is good, and for good may it be. May the merciful one make it turn out for good. Seven times may it be decreed from heaven that it is good and shall be."

Then Reb Zalman began to recite the words of the Psalm *You have turned my sackcloth into dancing.* And after this he related his dream. He said: "I felt my time had come and the

Hevra Kadisha was surrounding my bed. I had said the *Viduy*, the confession, and was ready to invite the *Malach Hamoves*, the Angel of Death, to do his work...quickly. Utilizing every Name of God I had learned, I effected the Unification and saw myself plunged into a torrent of white light before Duma, the Angel of the Grave, even before he had a chance to interrupt me and ask me his questions, for I wished nothing else but to be drawn into the very body of the One who is the source of all blessings. Like a drop merging with the ocean, I wished to be assimilated into *Ein Sof.*

"Wave after wave of swirls interrupted the *mikveh* of the River of Light. Each time my head bobbed up from that river, I saw another image. Sometimes it seemed to be that all of mankind was actually connected. And what seems to us to be the upper part of a person, that which stands out and makes him look separate, was only an appendage of that one being which we all are underneath the surface.

"I saw myself from time to time rousing the somnolent parts of myself. Some of them woke up with smiles, some woke up startled, and others were angry and cursed for having been woken up from their long sleep and because they wished to stay in their separateness. And responding to their anger, I found myself getting angry as well. And only the next wave of the River of Light washed away my anger and carried it out to sea.

"Then another wave came, and as I emerged from the river every good deed I had ever done in my life surrounded me, tempting me with pride, and I did not know what to do with them. But suddenly I saw Melchizedek, the King of Salem and the High Priest on high. I said to him: 'Please, take my *mitzvot* and offer them up. They are not for me, but for the Holy One, blessed be He.' And Melchizedek lifted up the *mitzvot* and as he did he lifted me up as well. And there, as he lifted me very high, the River of Light bathed my soul once more.

"All during that time I heard the surging sound of a *bat kol*, a heavenly voice, although I could not make the words out. But this time, as I was about to plunge again into the next wave of the River of Light, I heard it but not very clearly. The voice said: *Whom shall I send and who shall go for us?* This time my mind did not merge with the River of Light, so painful was the cry of the *Shekhinah* with those words. And before I knew it, I cried out hoarsely: 'I will go.'

"I followed the sound I heard, trying to reach its source, and before long I found myself before a Vale of Tears, smokestacks with blue smoke curling up to heaven in my father's town of Oswiecim. Countless people were crying out *Shema Yisrael* as their last outcry. And all the while the *Shekhinah* was wailing and wailing but the Omnipotent One did not give Her any power to stop what was happening. Again I cried out 'I will go,' thinking I was to join the martyrs.

"In the next wave, the *Shekhinah* repeated Her question with urgent clarity, and this time I responded with a clear voice. I was carried still further into the future and saw a country in which many Jews made their home. And in that country there were Jews who, if they received any Torah at all, received only the outer trappings of *Yiddishkite,* and none of its inner joys. And my soul was attracted to go there. And there I saw myself studying in a *Yeshivah* where the joy and power of the Torah had not been lost, and with others who had responded to the call and kept looking for that which was lacking in all of that country.

"And then I found myself faced with an awakening in which I saw the River of Light once more and my path to which I had become pledged, running beside it. And I started to look for a way in which I could fulfill the task that I had undertaken. And that path led me to a *Beit Midrash,* and when I entered there I saw that the shelves were lined with books. And I opened those books and saw that each one contained a script for a *Tzaddik* who lived in a different time. There was a wonderful script about how to be a *Tzaddik* in the time of Rabbi Akiba and Rabbi Shimon bar Yohai; a wonderful one about how to be a *Tzaddik* in Medieval Spain, such as Yehuda Halevi; another that spoke of how to be a *Tzaddik* in early Germany, such as Judah the Pious. The volume of the script of the Ari still had the letters dancing in it. And there was one about how to be a *Tzaddik* in the time of the Baal Shem, but when I came to the book of how to be a *Tzaddik* in my own time and opened it, I found, to my horror, that it was blank. There was no script.

"Then I called out and I said: *'Ribbono Shel Olam*, I have volunteered and said that I would come and serve. But I do not know how to serve you in this century. So much has changed. So few of the things that were guidelines in the past can be of help to me today.' But there was only silence. And at that I fell into great terror, and I began to cry.

"Then I began to count all the books on the shelves. And when I had counted them all I found that there were six hundred and twenty books, one for each of the six hundred and thirteen *mitzvot* and one for each of the seven *mitzvot* of the *Rabbanim*. And I opened up each and every one of those books, and searched each of those ways, but none of them held the script I was searching for. At last I came back to the blank book and I studied it more closely. And so I discovered that one thing had been written on it—my name. Then I realized that I myself would have to inscribe the pages of the book open before me. I looked for quill and ink but learned that each page had to be written by a mixture of tears, sweat and blood, mixed with black bile—melancholia. Then I began to cry, sweat, and pierced my finger for blood and began to write. But I discovered that if the ingredient of joy was missing, the letters would soon fade and the page would become blank again. That is how I learned I had to add joy to that mixture, for only then would the ink be permanent."

Just then Reb Zalman stopped speaking and looked up and found himself standing before the *Beit Din*. And he was silent for a long time, but at last he said: "Now tell me, will the letters that I write in that book lead me to *Gan Eden* or will they bring me to *Gehenna?* Will I be able to fulfill that for which I offered my soul, or will I in my eagerness drag myself and those who follow me into the abyss?"

And when Reb Zalman had said this, the members of the *Beit Din* realized how complex was the matter and how heavy the weight of their decision. And they consulted together in whispers for a very long time, but they could not reach a conclusion. Therefore they asked the two scribes, Reb Hayim Elya and Reb Sholem, to join them. And they continued to consult for another two hours, until three hours had passed, and all that time Reb Zalman stood before them, his head sunk on his chest, and it seemed to him that his soul hung in the balance by a slender thread.

At last the *Beit Din* reached a decision, and Reb Shmuel Leib spoke for the court and said: "As to where the path you have taken will lead you, we are unable to say. All we can tell you is this: It is clearly destined that you will live until you have finished inscribing every page of that book. May He who gives peace to those who are far and near guard you well until that day and guard your soul in the days that follow."

At that point they all started to chant the *Hatavat Halom*, and Reb Zalman went to *daven* singing "Haleluyah" with a strange melody and a strange rhythm which none of the Hasidim had ever heard.

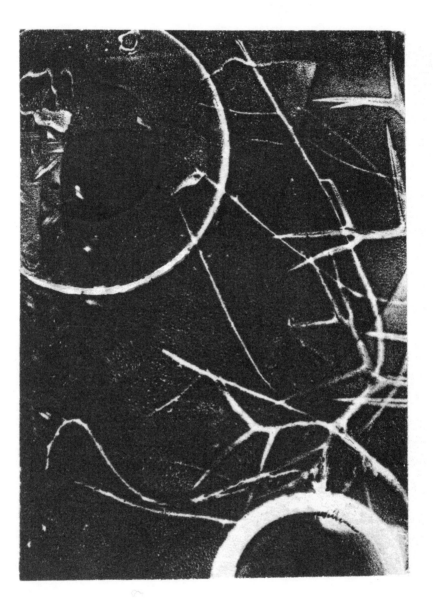

The Maiden of the Spring

In a forest outside of a small town in Poland there was a spring. But even though the waters of that spring were pure, none would dare to drink from it. For it was said that a spirit could be heard crying there at night, the ghost of a Jewish maiden who lost her life there to the Cossacks during a Pogrom. And they said as well that in the place where her blood flowed, the spring began to flow. So it was that none dared go near the spring at night.

Two Hasidim of Reb Zalman, known as Feivel the Dark and Feivel the Light, because their beards were black and white, were spending the night in that town while on a journey. They did not know about the spring, and since it was the eve of a fast day, they sought to find a *mikveh* in which to immerse themselves. Feivel the Light remembered having seen the spring as they journeyed through the forest. They made their way there by the light of the moon, which was almost full that night. All that each one carried was a *tallis*.

When the two Feivels reached the spring, they each put on the *tallis*, covering not only their shoulders, but also their heads, the way Reb Zalman did. But just as they were about to pray, they heard the sound of crying nearby them, which filled them with both pity and terror. For there was something other-worldly about that sound that chilled them to the bone. Feivel the Light was so frightened that he wanted to run away at once, but Feivel the Dark insisted that they protect themselves with prayer. For if their faith remained firm, the Holy One would see to it that they would come to no harm.

Then the two Hasidim began to pray with all their heart. And the instant they began to chant, by heart, the prayers they knew so well, the crying ceased. And when they finished praying, it did not resume. And when Feivel the Light saw this, his faith in the power of prayer was strengthened for good. Then Feivel the Dark undressed and went to the spring and immersed himself. But no sooner did he slip into the water than a great grief overtook him. He became very sad and began to cry. Feivel the Light was very confused, and begged the other Feivel to tell him what was wrong. But Feivel the Dark could not stop crying until he had stepped out of the waters of the spring.

When he finally stood again on the shore, all the grief departed from Feivel the Dark, as if he had never experienced it. This truly amazed them both, and finally Feivel the Dark begged the other to immerse himself as well, to see if his reaction was unique, or if it were somehow caused by the waters of that spring. At last Feivel the Light found the courage to step into those waters, and even before he had fully immersed himself he was so filled with sadness that he was choked with tears. Then he did not hesitate, but dipped and ran from that spring as fast as he could. And after that the two Hasidim hurriedly dressed and made their way back to town without speaking so much as a single word.

The next day the two Feivels discussed what had happened to them with the innkeeper with whom they were staying. The innkeeper was horrified that they had gone there, and begged their forgiveness for not telling them about it. He admitted that he tried to put it out of his mind, since it frightened him so much. And then he told the two Hasidim the tale of the maiden of the spring who had lost her life there.

This story was so sad that it caused both Hasidim to become filled with grief again, as they had been the night before. And in the presence of the innkeeper they both wept.

The next day the two Hasidim continued their journey. And when they had returned to Zholkiev, they told Reb Zalman about their frightening experience at the spring. When Reb Zalman heard about it, he too shared their grief. For since the two Feivels had heard about the maiden of the spring, their lives had taken on a cast of sadness such as was not characteristic of them. Reb Zalman thought about the spring all that week, and on Thursday morning, when the Sabbath was approaching, he told the two Feivels to join for the Midnight Lament at that spring rather than in the *Beit Midrash*.

The two were confused by this sudden decision, but they both agreed to go at once, for the story of that sad maiden had begun to haunt their lives, and they had faith that if anyone could help in this matter, it was Reb Zalman, who opened himself to the spirits as much as he did to the living.

The three Hasidim arrived at the spring shortly before nightfall. Reb Zalman had them all sit nearby the spring and cover their heads with their *tallisim*. Then he called upon the maiden of the spring to appear, to reveal herself to them. And lo and behold, before long, her voice, like a low wind, reached them and identified herself. The two Feivels each shook beneath their *tallisim*, but Reb Zalman was filled with certainty. He asked the maiden to tell them her story, and when the two Feivels heard about the terrible manner in which she had lost her life, before she, who had been snatched from the *Huppah* by the Cossacks, had known her hour of joy, they began to choke with tears. But Reb Zalman did not let himself dissolve into grief. Instead he asked the wandering spirit why it remained so close to that spring. And the spirit replied that the spring had indeed come into being as a result of her murder, but it was not really a pure water spring. Instead it was a spring of tears of all of the griefs of those who had their blood spilled in that land. And so it would remain until the spring was purified.

This was what Reb Zalman was waiting for. He quickly asked to know how the spring could be purified, and the spirit told him that if the body of a pure man who had died was washed there, the spring would be restored to purity and the spirit could depart. And when the maiden's spirit had revealed this, it disappeared.

Then Reb Zalman told the others to take the *tallis* from their heads, and asked if they had heard the maiden as clearly as he had. And they each confirmed that they had heard every word. And none of them doubted that the spring might be purified in that way.

Later that year Reb Zalman was called to the deathbed of one of his Hasidim. This young Hasid had postponed marriage due to his diligence and love for the Torah. But because his life was still unfulfilled, he found it difficult to take leave of this world without having tasted his hour of joy.

When Reb Zalman stood before him, the Hasid revealed his bitterness at having to take leave of this world in a way that made him feel cheated. Reb Zalman said: "Fear not, your hour of joy is not lost." And the dying Hasid reached out to this spark of hope, and said: "How can this be?" And Reb Zalman told him the tale of the maiden of the spring. And when the Hasid heard this tale, he called in the brethren of the *Hevra Kadisha* and said to them: "Please, I ask you, a kindness of truth. See to it that my body is immersed in the spring of the maiden, for that must be my *mikveh.*"

So it was that they agreed to let it be done. And when the body of the young man touched those waters, a great sigh rose up, which was heard by all those present. And after that the waters of the spring became pure, and the spring itself became the most famous *mikveh* in all of Poland, to which Jews came from all over the land for purification and healing, and brides, in particular, to prepare for their nuptials.

CROSSING THE SEA

O|ne day Reb Zalman spoke to his Hasidim of the passage at the Red Sea. He said: "The Talmud tells us that even the maidservant among the children of Israe' who crossed the Red Sea saw more than Ezekiel in his vision. How is this possible? Because the six hundred thousand Israelites who gathered at the shore of the Red Sea bore the souls of those created on the sixth day of creation. For, if the truth be known, each of those souls is attached to one of the six hundred thousand letters of the Torah. And if even a single Israelite had been left behind, that letter of the Torah would have been lost. And without it the Torah would not be complete, and could not serve us as a perfect mirror of truth.

"So it was that as they stepped into the sea, each and every Israelite had a vision, in which they had revealed to them the Mysteries of Creation, and relived the moment of the conception of their soul. And at the same time they were shown the root which linked them to one of the letters of the Torah, and it was then that they learned which letter this was. So too were they able to see once again the primordial light that still existed then, for if the truth be known it was not lost,

as some have said. Rather, it was hidden by the Holy One, so
that only those worthy of seeing it would have it revealed to
them. But so filled with love for His people was the Holy One,
blessed be He, at the time of the crossing at the Red Sea, that
he let every one of the children of Israel perceive that long
lost light.

"And what did they see in that light? Like Adam, they
saw from one end of the world to the other, and the future
generations were made as known to them as those of the past.
And this was true of the lowest among them, even the maid-
servant, as I have said. For it is a secret known to very few
that when the waters of the Red Sea parted, the Holy One
filled the empty space with the primordial light, which is the
pure essence of His love. And as they became immersed in
the light, each and every one had a vision that revealed even
more than Ezekiel had seen in the *Merkavah*. And as they
passed through the River of Light, the Israelites had revealed
to them the light of Sinai, which is the light of the Torah. For
the primordial light has been preserved in the Torah, since
that is where the Holy One hid it."

Here Reb Zalman stopped, and all of the Hasidim felt as
if they too had stepped into the River of Light. For a while
there was silence, as each contemplated the mysteries Reb
Zalman had revealed from on high. Then Reb Sholem asked
Reb Zalman if the vision of each man and woman was the
same, or if it was different for every one of them. Reb Zalman
grew solemn when he heard this, and said: "Tell me first how
many of you would have been willing to immerse yourselves
in the water of the Red Sea until it reached your neck?" And
all of the Hasidim turned to each other, for they had never
considered this question before. Some of them were certain
they would enter the waters, while others were not so sure.
Then Reb Zalman said: "There are some things that can be
revealed by word of mouth, and there are some things that
can only be known firsthand. Therefore, those of you who
wish to know for certain what you would have done should
do as I say: Take off your prayer sash and blindfold yourselves with it. Then take hands and let me lead you."

And even though some of them were uncertain and some were even afraid, all of the Hasidim took off their prayer sashes and wrapped them around their eyes, and taking the hand of those next to them, let Reb Zalman lead them in a line outside the House of Study, into the nearby forest. Then, unknown to them, Reb Zalman led them to a spring in that forest, which they used as a *mikveh*. That pure spring murmured with the sound of flowing water. When they stood around it, Reb Zalman told the blind-folded Hasidim to listen very carefully and they would be able to hear the waters of the Red Sea. The Hasidim listened intently, aided by the fact that they could not see. And because their hearing was more keen, the murmuring of the spring seemed to grow louder, until it resembled the sound of waves crashing at the shore. Then, all at once, they heard a terrible noise from behind—the sound of approaching hooves. And one and all they knew what it was—the Egyptians. Then a great fear seized them, and Reb Zalman said: "There is only one way to go—forward into the waters of the sea. Have faith that the Holy One will protect you and that the waters will part." And Reb Zalman started to lead them forward. But some of them held back, for they were filled with fear and trembling. And others said: "Let us turn back!" And another group said: "No, let us throw ourselves upon the mercy of God and go into the sea." And still others said: "There's no going forward and no turning back. Therefore let us stay and fight!" And still others said: "Let us cry out against them so terribly that they will take fright and turn back."

Then Reb Zalman replied to them. To those who wanted to turn back, he said: *"For whereas ye have seen the Egyptians today, ye shall see them no more forever."* And to those ready to throw themselves into the sea, he said: *"Stand still and see the salvation of the Lord."* To those who said they wanted to fight, he said: *"The Lord will fight for you."* And to those who wanted to cry out, he said: *"And ye shall hold your peace."*

Then one Hasid among them, whose name was Reb Nachshon, took heart and stepped into the waters of the spring, which rose up to his mouth. And in that moment they heard the waters rush away, and knew with certainty that they had parted. And all of those standing on the shore were suddenly filled to overflowing with song, and they sang out in unison the Song at the Sea. And as they sang, Reb Zalman led them forward, into the spring. And each one, as he was immersed there, recovered his soul's memory of crossing the sea. And every memory was a little different, for every soul is linked to a different letter. Yet every one of their souls had been among the six hundred thousand at the sea. And therefore they each needed to be faithful to their own memory so that they could speak their own truth in words that come from the heart. And by the time Reb Zalman had led them back to the House of Study and they removed the sashes, each and every one of them knew for himself the answer to Reb Sholem's question.

THE TALE OF THE SUKKAH

One day Reb Hayim Elya came to visit Reb Zalman and found him sitting on a rafter of his *Sukkah*. Hayim Elya asked him what he was doing there, and Reb Zalman replied: "The rule is that the roof of the *Sukkah* be loose enough so that one can see the sky, yet thick enough that no one space may be left uncovered. I saw a place where too much sun was shining through, and I realized that it gave me an opportunity to serve."

Just then Reb Zalman happened to notice from his vantage point that a bird's nest in a nearby tree had slipped and was on the verge of falling, with the fledgings in it. Then, without hesitation—for it is written that if an opportunity to perform a *mitzvah* presents itself, one must not be slow in performing it—Reb Zalman climbed down from the roof of the *Sukkah* and hurried to the tree in which the nest teetered so precariously. Hayim Elya gave him a boost, and Reb Zalman climbed into the tree. Then Hayim Elya handed him a stick and with it he pushed the nest back into a safe place. But while he was perched there, Reb Zalman saw in the distance a young boy running down the road, who seemed to be distraught. Then he climbed down from the tree and he and Hayim Elya hurried off together to see what was wrong.

When they reached the young boy, Reb Zalman recognized him as the son of the miller, who was known as a drunkard and a dangerous enemy of the Jews. The boy was hysterical and almost incoherent, but the Hasidim were able to discern that something had happened to his father. They followed the boy to the mill, and there they found that the miller had slipped while in a drunken state and his leg had fallen beneath the millstone and was in danger of being crushed. Reb Zalman and Hayim Elya quickly pulled him out from under the stone, and Hayim Elya ran off to bring a doctor. Meanwhile Reb Zalman did everything he could to comfort the miller. To distract him from his pain, he pointed out some birds flying with bits of straw in their beaks which they had picked up from the floor of the mill. When the doctor came he examined the miller's leg, and told him that had the Hasidim not called upon him to come there quickly, he would surely have lost the leg, which now was just as surely to be saved. And the miller was deeply grateful for the help of the Hasidim, and as a result an enemy of the Jews became a loyal friend.

As Reb Zalman and Hayim Elya walked back to the *Sukkah* Reb Zalman noted that one *mitzvah* leads to another, and that if he had not sat upon the roof of the *Sukkah*, he would not have known that the fledgings and the miller were in need of help. That reminded them that the open space in the roof of the *Sukkah* must be repaired. But when they reached the *Sukkah* both were amazed to find that the birds had deposited straw from the mill on the roof of the *Sukkah*, which had sufficiently closed off the open space making it a fully proper *Sukkah*. And both Hasidim recognized that in this way the Holy One, blessed be He, had acknowledged the *mitzvot* they had undertaken to perform.

TABERNACLE OF PEACE

That *Sukkos* Reb Zalman gave his *D'var Torah* in the *Sukkah* behind his house, into which all of his Hasidim crowded. His subject that year was the Tabernacle of Peace which descends around the earth whenever the *Shekhinah* descends from on high to embrace her children, Israel. And in the shelter of that Tabernacle, the world is awash in its glory. That is truly the time of abundance.

Reb Zalman said: "Now when is it that the *Shekhinah* descends? Her visits take place on every *Shabbas* and holy day. That is why those days are so sacred—for the Holy One saw fit to permit His bride, the *Shekhinah,* to take leave of the world above and embrace her children in the world below. Therefore we embrace these days ourselves, so that our embrace may meet that of the *Shekhinah.* And in the shelter of that embrace our lives are rocked as if in a cradle of peace."

Later that day Reb Zalman and Reb Hayim Elya found themselves alone in the *Sukkah*. And Hayim Elya said: "Rebbe, tell me more about this Tabernacle of Peace, for while you spoke it was almost as if I could visualize it. Why, it was almost as if I saw one corner of the heavenly *Sukkah* planted above this very *Sukkah* of yours; as if the *Shekhinah* had reached down and embraced us. Tell me, please, why is it that we cannot hold on to this Tabernacle of Peace and make it remain with us all the time?"

Reb Zalman laughed when Hayim Elya said this, and then he said: "Know, Hayim Elya, that the *Sukkah* of the Tabernacle of Peace is bound to this world by four golden threads. Those threads are as thin as the thinnest thread, so that they barely can be seen glinting in the sunlight. But they are there. Yet at the same time, they are fragile, they are only threads. And if we tried to hold on to them, they would simply break."

Now, strangely enough, Hayim Elya was not disappointed, but even more intrigued. And he said: "Are you saying, then, Rebbe, that it might be possible to hold on to one of those golden threads in a gentle way without causing it to break?" And Reb Zalman replied: "It is precisely to be able to do this that Moses received the Torah on Sinai. And this is the ultimate secret that the Torah is able to teach. For as long as we are in that Divine Presence, our lives will be filled with blessings, for the *Shekhinah* is the source of all blessings in this world, at the behest of the Holy One, blessed be He."

Hayim Elya quickly responded: "Tell me, Rebbe, how is it possible to accomplish this? For now that you have spoken I have visualized the golden thread, which even now I see not far above your head. And it reaches up into the highest heavens. Even now I have traced the end that is tied to this earth to the very fringes of your *tallis,* in this room." And Reb Zalman looked down in amazement, and saw that there was indeed a golden thread entwined around one of the *tsitsis* of his prayer shawl. And it was also true that this thread ascended from there as high as the eye could see, and, no doubt, much further. And suddenly Reb Zalman himself had a great insight, and he said to Hayim Elya with joy, "In this very moment, Hayim Elya, it has been revealed to me that the thread remains bound as long as we continue to be engaged in the discussion of Torah, as we are now. This is what King David discovered, and thus he was able to stave off the Angel of Death when he discovered that the angel was destined to take him on the Sabbath. So he spent every moment of every *Shabbas* in the study of the Torah, and the Angel of Death was unable to approach him. Only by creating a diversion did the Angel finally trick him out of his room, or else he might still be alive to this day. Yes, our salvation lies in the Torah in more ways than we might imagine."

So it was that long after the sun had set at the end of *Sukkos,* Reb Zalman and Hayim Elya continued to speak of the Torah in its myriad forms. And all that time the golden thread, now glowing in the dark, remained coiled around one fringe of Reb Zalman's *tallis.* And only after the sun had risen, and they had finished praying *Shahareis,* did they bid farewell to the *Shekhinah* as she gently lifted the Tabernacle of Peace from this world. And by then Reb Zalman had come to understand in the most elementary way the secret of the *Shekhinah.* And as the two of them sat together, awed by all they had witnessed, Reb Zalman said: "All that we have discovered in these hours under the *Sukkah* can be expressed in the simplest way. And this, above all, is what I have learned: That the essence of the *Shekhinah* is called forth through every crown and every letter of the Torah, whenever it is opened and read, or even when it is simply discussed. For as long as the words of the Torah are spoken in this world, the golden threads will remain coiled in the fringes of our *tallisim,* as long as they are being worn. During every such moment the *Shekhinah* is permitted to remain here, among us, and in this way the world is able to remain sheltered in her Tabernacle of Peace. And that, Hayim Elya, is the answer to your question."

THE SEVEN SHEPHERDS

On the eve of *Hosha'na Rabbah*, the seventh and last day of *Sukkos*, Reb Zalman and seven of his Hasidim were sitting together in the *Sukkah*. Nearby there was a brook that wound its way through the field. And on the far side of the brook there were many willow trees. That night Reb Zalman directed the Hasidim to take torches and go across the brook, and there to cut down seven willow branches each—instead of the usual five.

The Hasidim departed at once, with Reb Shmuel Leib leading them to the bank. Although night had fallen, the moon was in its last quarter, and the water of the brook glittered in the moonlight. When they came to the shore, Reb Sholem said: "Should we cross the brook by stepping on stones, or should we go through the water?" For they were on a sacred task, and every step they took mattered. Reb Yosele argued that they should cross on the rocks, for the waters of the Red Sea had parted before the children of Israel and they had walked upon the rocks at the bottom. However, Reb Hayim Elya argued against this position, reminding them that *Hosha'na Rabbah* was a very solemn day, on which the final decision about a man's life that was signed on *Yom Kippur* was finally sealed in the Book of Life. Thus it was the very last time to change an ill fate. And since the waters of the brook were pure, running waters, to cross them would be to immerse themselves once more in a *mikvah*, and thus offer themselves one last chance to purify their souls.

The Hasidim decided in favor of Hayim Elya's interpretation, and they all stepped into the waters of the brook and crossed it. And for the short time they were in the water, they felt the cold currents swirling around them, and it seemed as if they were indeed being purified. Then they cut down the willow branches, seven for each one, and crossed back to the other shore.

When they returned, Reb Zalman directed Reb Sholem to read *Devarim*, the fifth book of Moses, from start to finish. And when the Hasidim heard it that night, complete in itself rather than in many small portions, they saw it in a new light, and its meaning in sum was even far greater than they had imagined. And Reb Zalman took over to read the last speech of Moses. And he read it as if Moses had addressed it to them that very day. And it seemed to the Hasidim as if the *Sukkah* was illumined by a light from within, and they saw the aura that is said to have surrounded Moses glowing like a pure flame from Reb Zalman's face.

Then Reb Zalman told the Hasidim to come to him, and one by one he took their willow branches and rolled them together and bound them with a leaf from a lulav frond. Then Reb Zalman handed the willows back to the Hasid, and when he did he seemed to look past him. Afterward the Hasidim said it was as if he were looking at the page inscribed in the Book of Life and reading what was written there.

Then Reb Zalman told the Hasidim to take up those willow branches and beat them against the floor seven times, instead of the usual five. The Hasidim were not familiar with this form of the *minhag*, but they did not question it. Each one beat the branches against the dirt floor of the *Sukkah*, and the seventh time they did it a vision took form before their eyes, and they suddenly found that they were able to see the demons of their own lives, the flaws that pursued them even into the most sacred moments. And when they saw those demons, they were horrified and filled with terror at the same time. And they cried out to Reb Zalman to save them from those demons which so tormented them.

Just then they heard voices outside the *Sukkah*, and seven Jews entered, all of estimable age. The Hasidim assumed that they were a group of visiting rabbis who had come to visit Reb Zalman on that holy night. Nor did Reb Zalman introduce them to his Hasidim; instead he caused them to be mortified by pointing out the demons that surrounded each and every one. Then there was a look of compassion on the faces of the seven visitors, and each of them went up to one of the seven Hasidim, took his willow broom, sweeping in front of that Hasid, turning the demons into angels; imperfect angels at first, with the seventh sweep making them worthy of the Divine Presence.

When the demons had all been turned into angels, the eyes of the ancient ones sparked with joy, and they nodded, took their leave, and departed. And when they were gone, the angels that had been as clear to the Hasidim as themselves all vanished, yet they still were aware of their invisible presence. For a long time the Hasidim were dumbfounded, and there was nothing but silence. Finally Reb Sholem found the courage to speak and asked to know who the visitors were. And Reb Zalman replied: "The Seven Shepherds— Abraham, Isaac, Jacob, Moses, Aaron, Joseph and David."

And that is how Reb Zalman's Hasidim learned the purpose of the ritual of beating the willow branches seven times on the morning of *Hosha'na Rabbah.*

THE TALE OF THE TALLIS

One day, after he had completed his *D'var Torah*, which had been on the subject of the virtues of the *tallis*, Reb Zalman asked his Hasidim if there were any questions they wanted to ask. Reb Sholem said: "Tell me, Rebbe, who was it who wore the first *tallis*?"

And Reb Zalman smiled a great smile, for that is exactly what he wanted to tell them, if only they would ask. And he said: "Abraham was the first to wear a *tallis*, of course. But it was not just any *tallis*, but a *tallis* woven out of light by the *Shekhinah*, and colored with the colors of the rainbow. And the center stripe of it was blue, the same blue as *tekehlet*, because that is the same blue that is found in the heavens. And that is why we were commanded to tie the *tsitsis* with a thread of that color—to make the link between the worlds above and below even more complete.

"Now the three angels who came to Abraham disguised as wanderers gave him that *tallis* as a gift after he made every effort to be a perfect host, despite the pain of his recent *bris*. And for Abraham that prayershawl was the most precious possession in the world, and that was indeed the case, for the

Torah had not been given yet, but remained in Paradise, although Abraham was permitted to read from it in his dreams.

"And Abraham wrapped himself in that *tallis* every time he prayed, day or night. And on his deathbed he bestowed this *tallis* upon Isaac. And had he not given it to his son, he would have been wrapped and buried in that *tallis*. And with the protection of that *tallis* he would have stepped directly before the *Pargod,* the Curtain that hangs before the Throne of Glory, on which all truths are to be found. But Abraham preferred to bequeath that wonderful *tallis* to this world. And in giving it to Isaac he set a pattern that has been continued among all the Children of Israel—not only to receive, but to transmit as well. And there is a great mystery here, for in letting it go to another we are able to keep it for ourselves all that much more.

"So it was that this *tallis* reached Jacob, and Joseph after him. And this was the coat of many colors of which the brothers of Joseph were so jealous, and for which they threw Joseph into a pit and sold him into slavery. But Jacob kept that *tallis* among his possessions, after his sons brought it back to him bloodied and torn, as proof that Joseph had lost his life, as they falsely claimed. And when he came down into Egypt with sixty-nine others, he brought that *tallis* with him, now restored, and gave it back to Joseph.

"Now Joseph had that *tallis* buried with him, for he knew, from prophetic dreams, that four hundred years of slavery would follow his reign, but that a Redeemer would arise after that, who would lead the Children of Israel to the Holy Land. And before he died he prayed to God that the *tallis* then be transmitted to this Redeemer. So it was that when Moses sought out the coffin of Joseph, and Serach bat Asher led him to where it had been sunk into the Nile, that he called for Joseph to arise and come with him. And because that enchanted *tallis* was buried with him, the whole coffin, which was made of gold, became light as a feather, and quickly rose to the surface.

"Now the Israelites carried the coffin of Joseph with them in the Wilderness for many years, but never did they open it. Yet among the commandments given to Moses at Mount Sinai in addition to the *mitzvot* was that he open the coffin of Joseph and take out the *tallis* that was in there, for it was a great gift to him from Joseph, and from the Holy One, as well, to confirm their Covenant. And when the time came for Moses to take his leave of the Children of Israel, he at last opened the coffin of Joseph and found the *tallis* of the *Shekhinah* inside, glowing with a wonderful aura. And when Moses put it on he understood completely the meaning of the words *wrapped in a garment of light.* And he understood as well how the Holy One, blessed be He, had wrapped himself in a garment of light at the beginning of time, in order to bring the world into being. And Moses bequeathed that *tallis* to all generations.

"And in this way that *tallis* came to Aaron, and to Pinhas, and to Eli, and to Samuel, and eventually to King David and King Solomon. And it was because of that enchanted prayer-shawl that King Solomon became a master of all the Mysteries. For when he wrapped himself in it anything he wished was at his command, its power now magnified by the glory of his forefathers, and the glory inherent in it because it was woven by the *Shekhinah.*"

Here Reb Zalman stopped, and for a long time the Hasidim were lost in imagining that divine *tallis.* But at last Hayim Elya felt the need to know more, and he said: "But Rebbe, what was the history of the *tallis* after that?"

And Reb Zalman said: "No one knows for certain what happened to that *tallis.* Some say it was destroyed along with the Temple, while others say the *Shekhinah* took it with her when she removed herself from this world due to the destruction of the Temple. Others say that it continued to be handed down, and in this way reached the true prophet or sage of each generation—it was the mantle worn by Elijah, which he bestowed on Elisha after him. And it also came into the possession of Shimon bar Yohai, who wore it during the thirteen years he spent in the cave. And it was because of the insights given to him by wearing that *tallis* that the Zohar is so filled with secret wonders, which were revealed to him.

"So too it is said that the *tallis* came into the possession of the Ari, who, when wrapping himself in it, had the vision of the Shattering of the Vessels and the Gatherings of the Sparks. And that is how he was able to bring this truth to this world, where the knowledge that we can repair that which is broken must give us great consolation. So too did the *tallis* reach the Maharal, Rabbi Judah Loew, and it was by wrapping himself in this *tallis* that he received the power to bring the Golem to life.

"Some say that after that the *tallis* was hidden in the same place as the clay of the Golem, the attic of the synagogue of the Maharal of Prague. But others say that it mysteriously came into the possession of the Baal Shem Tov, who received it from the son of Reb Adam, who had been commanded by his father to give it to Israel ben Eliezer, the boy who became the Baal Shem Tov. And some say that the Baal Shem concealed the *tallis* in the side of a mountain, while others insist that he gave it to his daughter, Odel, who bequeathed it to her daughter, Feige, who in turn gave it to her son, Reb Nachman of Bratslav."

Here Reb Zalman again stopped. And his Hasidim were breathless. For Reb Nachman had lived only a generation before their own. And had the enchanted *tallis* been lost so near to their own time? All of the Hasidim begged Reb Zalman to tell them if there were any more known of the history of that *tallis*. And at last Reb Zalman said: "Some say that Reb Nachman was the last mortal who will wear that *tallis* until the time of Messiah ben David. While others insist that it will continue to be handed down to the *Tzaddik ha-Dor* of every generation, until the time of the coming of the Messiah."

"Please, tell us Rebbe," Hayim Elya begged, "tell us which of these opinions is the right one?" And Reb Zalman looked solemn, and then he beckoned for the Hasidim to come with him. And he led them into his study, and there he opened his chest and a blinding light rose up that filled their eyes with glory.

NEITHER A TALLIS, NOR A COAT

One day, during a *D'var Torah*, Reb Zalman said to his Hasidim: "It is our duty, as Jews, to honor each and every one of the six hundred and thirteen *mitzvot* to the best of our ability. But know that every Jew finds one *mitzvah*, in particular that he loves, although which *mitzvah* differs for everyone. For me it is the *mitzvah* of *Shabbas* that I am drawn to above all the others, while for Hayim Elya it is the *mitzvah* to be fruitful and multiply that beckons him, perhaps because it is the first, but more so because he knows that creation is the most important gift. For Shmuel Leib it is the *mitzvah* of the *Mezzuzah* that matters the most, and each time he touches it he recites the *Shema* in full, exactly as it is written on the parchment within. And Reb Sholem—for Reb Sholem the *mitzvah* that means the most is that of the *tsitsis.*"

Now Reb Sholem had always loved the *mitzvah* of the *tsitsis,* but he had never realized that he loved it above all of the other *mitzvot.* Yet now that Reb Zalman had pointed it out, he saw how true it was with great clarity. And he was grateful to Reb Zalman for this insight, and after that he honored the *mitzvah* with even greater intensity. And he tried to think of a way to thank Reb Zalman. So it was that he decided to make Reb Zalman a coat cut like a *tallis,* with four corners. Of course such a coat would not be accepted as a *tallis,* after all, since it was not made of the same material as a prayershawl, but it would still give honor to the *mitzvah,* the way it was intended to, by reminding of it each time the coat was worn.

So it was that Reb Sholem took great care in making the coat, for he was the finest tailor in all of Zholkiev. And with every stitch that he sewed, he meditated upon the *mitzvah* of the *tallis.* It took a long time for that coat to be completed, an entire summer. And Reb Sholem brought it as a gift just as the first chills of autumn were beginning to be felt. Reb Zalman was astonished by the gift, and as he accepted it, he put it on. Suddenly he turned away, holding the front *tsitsis* in his hands, and spoke as if reporting a conversation. "Is it a coat? Is it a *tallis?* Yes, it's a coat. No, it's a *tallis.* It has *tsitsis,* it's a *tallis.* Whoever heard of a coat with *tsitsis?*" At this strange dialogue, from one mouth, Reb Sholem was mortified, for he thought that Reb Zalman was mocking him.

Reb Zalman saw that Reb Sholem's face had begun to grow long, and he said: "Is anything wrong, Sholem?" And Reb Sholem admitted that he felt that perhaps the Rebbe was mocking him, teasing him about it like some pious people who came into his shop. And Reb Zalman said: "Not at all, Sholem, not at all. I was merely reporting what I overheard said between Gabriel and Michael." And Reb Sholem said to Reb Zalman: "What do you mean? There is nobody else among us." Reb Zalman replied: "That is true—I was just reporting what I heard among the angels." "Is that all that the angels had to say?" said Reb Sholem, aghast. "No," said Reb Zalman with a great smile, "one also said to the other that even the Holy One, blessed be He, delighted in the sight of that coat. And the other replied that he had heard it said from behind the *Pargod* that the *kavanah* of Reb Sholem was so perfect as he sewed that coat, that each stitch he took sewed another stitch in the robe of the *Shekhinah* ."

When Reb Zalman said this, Reb Sholem cried tears of joy in profusion. And after that Reb Zalman was often seen wearing that garment, which was neither a *tallis*, nor a coat. And all who saw him wearing it were reminded of the *mitzvah* that meant so much to Reb Sholem.

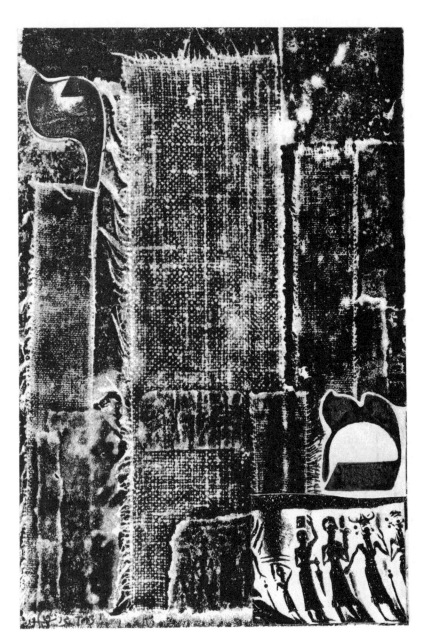

THE TALE OF THE SHROUD

One morning Reb Zalman sent for the *Hevra Kadisha* and told them it was necessary to exhume the body of a tailor who had been buried only the day before. The brethren were most amazed at this request, for such a thing had rarely, if ever, been done, and not in their lifetimes. But Reb Zalman insisted on it and his ruling was accepted as final.

When it was done, the people discovered that the shroud of the tailor was immaculate in every respect, except for one piece three inches long that was sewn onto the bottom of the shroud—that part was already full of maggots and worms, even though the burial had only taken place two days before. The people gasped to see this, and wondered how such a thing could have occurred. Reb Zalman immediately ordered the attached piece to be cut off and burned, and its ashes to be buried outside the fence. This was carried out at once, and the tailor was reburied with proper ritual.

Afterward there was great curiosity among the people as to how Reb Zalman had known to exhume the tailor, and as to the strange corruption of the hem of the shroud. But no one dared to ask Reb Zalman about it, and neither did he offer an explanation to anyone, even to the Gabbai of the *Hevra Kadisha*.

One year passed, and the time came for the *Yahrtzeit* of the tailor. And Reb Zalman, who had been silent about the subject all year, called the *Hevra Kadisha* together to observe the *Yahrtzeit* by learning a chapter of Mishna for the benefit of the tailor's soul. For "Mishna" and "*neshamah*" are both formed by the same letters. And as they made *L'hayim* over brandy and honeycake, Reb Zalman said: "On the night following his burial, the spirit of the tailor came to me in a dream and begged me to save him from demons who gave him no rest. He refused to depart unless I gave my word to have him exhumed. This I did, though I did not know why. As you know, we discovered the corruption of the hem. I too wondered at the meaning of this. Then, the following night, the soul of the tailor returned in a dream and thanked me. I said to him: 'Tell me, please, about the piece that was sewn onto the bottom of the shroud, and how the rest of the shroud protected you.' Then the tailor told me this tale:

"While he was still living, a man had come to him with the coat of a Russian priest. The man gave the coat to the tailor, and told him he could keep it on the condition that the man never saw it again. The tailor accepted the coat, noticed that it had a fine linen lining, cut out that lining and sewed it into a shroud for himself. But finding that it was three inches too short, he hemmed it with a piece he had taken from a customer, the part left over from a shroud he had made for him.

"After his death, the tailor's soul learned the true history of the lining of that coat, which now served as his shroud. For the man who had given it to him had a son-in-law who had once worn it while parading up and down the street three times. And why had his son-in-law, a learned and righteous man, done such a thing? In the synagogue his son-in-law had encountered a man who was crying because his family was being held hostage by a landlord, and were in danger of losing their lives unless the landlord received in full the three hundred rubles that the man owed him.

"The righteous son-in-law did not have that much money, but such a sum had been pledged to him as a dowry. Not wanting to ask his own father-in-law, he went to the richest man in town, who happened to be a *Misnagid,* and asked to borrow that amount. Now this man lost no chance to discredit the Hasidim.

"And it happened that a Russian priest had once left his coat as a pledge on a loan and had never redeemed it. And the rich man told the son-in-law that not only would he lend money to him, but he would give it to him outright if only he ould walk back and forth in the coat three times—and vow, as well, never to reveal the true reason to anyone. Then the righteous son-in-law had done this abhorrent deed, and when he was seen walking in the street in that coat, all assumed that he had lost his mind. Afterward it took him many years to dispel that impression, but never did he reveal the true reason for having worn that coat, no matter how many times he had been asked.

"But the father-in-law of the Hasid feared that coat, which still hung in the closet. Therefore he took it to the tailor and gave it away. And the tailor, being ignorant of the history of that coat, used of its lining for his shroud. The holy and secret deed had so suffused the coat with merit that the demons were unable to approach him. Thus it protected him like an amulet in which the Name is inscribed. But through the three inches of the material he had kept instead of returning to the customer, demons were able to torment him. That is why the tailor's soul came to me, and that is why the three inches were already putrid after only two days.

"And when that part had been severed, the power of the *mitzvah* continued to protect the tailor's soul until it threaded its way to Paradise. And there the soul learned that its companion there was to be none other than the righteous son-in-law, when his time would come to take leave of the world. And today those two are companions in paradise, residing among the souls of the righteous, devoting every day to unraveling the mysteries of the Torah."

THE ASHES OF THE RED HEIFER

E ver since the days of the Baal Shem Tov, Hasidim had made use of several means of purifying themselves. They had fasted, said psalms, and immersed themselves in the *Mikvah*. But in the century following the great pogroms, Reb Zalman began to feel that the world had become so impure that these methods of purification were not sufficient, and that a more powerful method was required.

Now in the days of Moses there had been such a method, which used the ashes of a red heifer in conjunction with pure waters. But the ritual had already ceased to be performed by the time of the Talmudic sages, for no red heifer had been found anywhere. The Talmud stated that such a heifer had to be pure red to the extent that not as many as two of its hairs were of any other color, and for more than fifteen hundred years no such heifer had been born. Therefore the ritual could not be performed.

Then it happened one year, in the days before *Yom Kippur*, that Reb Zalman had a long and vivid dream. In it one of Reb Zalman's Hasidim, Reb Moshe, who was a farmer, had a heifer born among his herd that was pure red. Reb Moshe decided that such an unusual heifer would be a fine gift for Reb Zalman, even though he was not aware of the ancient custom involving the red heifer, for he was not a learned man. So he brought the heifer to Reb Zalman's house and gave it to him.

Now when Reb Zalman saw that red heifer, he was incredulous, for how long had it been since such a red heifer had been born? He examined it closely and confirmed that not even a single hair was of another color. And Reb Zalman thanked Reb Moshe for the gift from the bottom of his heart. For then Reb Zalman knew that the red heifer was a sign from heaven that he had been right in believing that a great impurity filled the world, and that the time had come to utilize the ritual of the ashes of the red heifer once again.

But Reb Zalman also knew that the birth of such a red heifer was itself a sign of the great purity of him to whom it had been born. And he wondered if there were some reason that Reb Moshe had been singled out. For Reb Zalman felt that his own merits alone were not enough to deserve such a great blessing, but that the merits of Reb Moshe combined with his own had made this possible.

So Reb Zalman asked Reb Moshe if he had ever performed any *mitzvah* that might be deemed exceptional. Reb Moshe thought about it for a long time, and at last he replied: "The only such *mitzvah* that I can think of concerns the serpent in the well." "And what was it that happened?" asked Reb Zalman, who was very curious indeed to hear this tale, for he had not forgotten the role of the serpent in the garden of Eden, nor the role of the pure water in the ritual of the ashes of the red heifer. And Reb Moshe said: "A serpent of the most poisonous type had made its nest in the pure water well from which my neighbors and I draw our water. It became impossible to go near the well, because of the danger. But no one was willing to descend into the well and clean out the nest of that serpent. At last I agreed that I would undertake to do it. So I climbed into the bucket and had myself lowered into the well. And this, Rebbe, is the strange part, which I have not revealed to anyone else—for when I reached the nest of the serpent, and held the slaughtering knife above it, it simply vanished into thin air!"

Now when Reb Zalman heard this, he almost jumped out of his seat. And the words began to rush from him, and he said: "That was no ordinary snake that had made its nest in your well, Moshe, it must have been the *Nakash Hakadmoni,* the Primal Serpent itself. And it was not your knife it escaped from, but from you—because of your great purity. For the Primal Serpent cannot bear to be in the presence of purity. It is you, then, that the Holy One, blessed be He, has selected to expel the impurity of evil from the world, and the birth of this red heifer confirms that. But tell me, of what birth is your family?" And Reb Moshe replied that he was a Cohen, and when Reb Zalman heard this, he said: "Let there be no doubt then that it is you, not I, whom the Holy One has selected to perform the priestly role in the ritual that uses the ashes of the red heifer. Since it is the role of the priest to perform every aspect of that ritual, go and slaughter this heifer and burn it until nothing remains but its ashes. And take care that not a single ash is lost, for every one is invaluable, and must be used with great care so that they can last at least a thousand years, as did the ashes of the first red heifer, that of Moses. And when the ashes are ready, bring also water from the well from which you expelled the serpent, for in this way the Holy One has directed us to use that water. And take care, Moshe, that everything retains its complete purity."

Now Reb Moshe was a simple farmer, but he did not doubt for a moment the words of Reb Zalman, for he had seen that serpent vanish with his own eyes. And he did as Reb Zalman told him, and took the great care in doing so that nothing became impure, and on the morning of *Erev Yom Kippur* he brought the ashes and the water to the home of Reb Zalman. And when Reb Zalman saw him, he embraced him with all his love, for he knew that the Holy One had given them a way to purify the world.

That *Yom Kippur* Reb Zalman added a new ritual to the service—he had Reb Moshe perform the ritual of the ashes of the red heifer on every person present there. For while it was true that the ritual would purify anyone who was impure, it was also true that the effect of the ashes on one pure would be to render him impure. But Reb Zalman did not worry about this. He reasoned that in that time everyone was in dire need of such purification, not merely the *Cohanim* or the High Priest. And even Reb Moshe was in need of the purifying effect, for he had descended far into the nest of the primal serpent. And the ritual of the ashes and the pure water, when done in conjunction with the *kavanah* that always accompanies *Yom Kippur* with its fasting and self purification, had the effect of purifying every Jewish soul in that synagogue. Just then Reb Zalman awoke, and much to his amazement found himself not in the synagogue, but at home, in his own bed. Still he felt like the burdens of a lifetime had been lifted and that the purity of God's Word shimmered in his very soul. And then he knew that in the world above the ashes of the red heifer had been prepared, and awaited the purification that must be made ready below.

Elijah's Disguise

During one of their travels together Reb Zalman and Reb Hayim Elya took a carriage from one town to the next. There was one other in that carriage, a poor man dressed in the clothes of a Gentile, who was asleep. Reb Zalman and Hayim Elya were discussing the meaning of the passage in Job, "and he disguiseth his face." Reb Zalman spoke of how many secrets are hidden, and must be ferreted out. He noted, for example, how Elijah can appear at any time in any place, always in disguise.

Here Hayim Elya raised another point: "But tell me, Rebbe, is it at least certain that Elijah will always appear in the clothes of a Jew?" And Reb Zalman shook his head and said: "Not at all. For the Holy One, blessed be He, sent Elijah into this world so that we would remain aware of *all* those around us, Jew or Gentile. Just as any Jew might be one of the *Lamed-vav Tzaddikim*, the Thirty-six Just Men, so is it possible that Elijah may be any man or woman at all, rich or poor, Jew or Gentile."

With these words echoing in his mind, Hayim Elya happened to glance at the sleeping Gentile. If what Reb

Zalman said was true, this man must be considered a possible Elijah as well, a thought that Hayim Elya found difficult to accept. Perhaps feeling the presence of Hayim Elya's stare, the other opened his eyes, and stared back at him. Hayim Elya nodded and greeted the man, who returned his greeting. Hayim Elya asked him what line of business he was in, and the Gentile said that he raised goats, and that he was traveling to the next town to sell goatskins. It was then that Hayim Elya noticed the bag of the old man, which he now saw was stuffed with goatskins.

Now Hayim Elya was a *sopher*, one who writes on parchment, which is made either from the skin of a sheep or a goat. Thus he asked the old man if he might look at one of the skins. Then the old man opened up his bag and took out the skin that lay on top. Hayim Elya turned it over, looking at the side opposite the skin, and he saw that it was the whitest skin he had ever seen, completely without blemish. He had never seen a skin like it in his life, for every other had some kind of imperfection in the grain or slight blemish. But that goatskin was perfectly white, immaculate. And Hayim Elya knew that he must make it his own, to use as a *qlaf* of parchment on which to write words of the Torah.

Hayim Elya showed the skin to Reb Zalman, who noted with a nod that it was exceptional. And Hayim Elya asked the old man how much he wanted for it. And the old man gave him a price that was ridiculous, far more than he could afford. This greatly distressed Hayim Elya, for he had already begun to imagine the dark outline of the letters against that pure white grain. And in despair he offered the old man all that he had in his leather purse, but no more. He did not specify the sum. And the old man looked up at him and smiled a peculiar smile, and agreed to this.

Then Hayim Elya opened up the purse and began to count out the coins. But instead of the handful of copper pennies he had been carrying, he found instead a large number of gold coins. Hayim Elya could not imagine from where they had appeared, and Reb Zalman too was astounded. Yet just then, when the miracle had occurred, Hayim Elya had agreed to give up all that his purse held, which he now recognized was worth far more than all the skins the old man was carrying with him. And in a state of great confusion, Hayim Elya turned over the bag of golden coins, and the old man told him that the goatskin was his to keep. Then he stuffed the bag of golden coins into his bag, and shouted to the driver of the carriage that he wanted to get out there, for he had reached his destination.

And while Hayim Elya and Reb Zalman watched in amazement, the old man leaped out and vanished into the forest. And Reb Zalman turned to Hayim Elya and said: "This teaches us two things—first, that in the eyes of the Lord, the words of the Torah are far more precious than a bag of gold, and second, that Elijah can truly come disguised as any Jew or Gentile."

When they returned to Zholkiev, Hayim Elya turned that white skin into a piece of the finest parchment. And he used that skin sparingly, not wasting a single inch. And the texts that he wrote on that skin for the *Mezzuzah* and *Tefillin* brought remarkable protection to those who possessed them, for on that parchment the words retained their full power, as they had at the time Moses received them on Mount Sinai. And that is why they were able to protect so well. Many lives were saved this way, and the time came when Hayim Elya and Reb Zalman both recognized that the benefits of that parchment were far greater than could be purchased with any bag of gold.

THE TALE OF THE WHITE GOAT

Now Reb Hayim Elya always wondered about the white goat that had supplied the pure white parchment he had purchased from Elijah, who had disguised himself as an old Gentile. For the strips of it he used for writing sacred texts demonstrated a remarkable amuletic power. And Hayim Elya wondered in particular if that goat had been raised in this world, or in *Gan Eden*.

On occasion Hayim Elya would mention this matter to Reb Zalman, and one day Reb Zalman said to him: "Why don't you take a piece of that pure parchment and place it beneath your pillow. And at the same time offer up a dream question, and perhaps you will come to learn something about that goat."

Now Hayim Elya did this, and offered up the dream question, and that night he dreamed that he was traveling down a long road, when he reached the gate of an orchard. In the dream he was hungry, thirsty and tired, and from the gate he could see all kinds of fruit trees and running streams inside that orchard. But when he tried the gate, he found that

it was locked. And as much as he cried out for someone inside
to come and open it, no one appeared.

Then, just as he was about to despair, Hayim Elya
glimpsed a white goat running out of the nearby forest and
around the wall that surrounded that orchard. In the dream
Hayim Elya followed the goat, in hope that it might show him
how to enter that orchard. And, indeed, this is what it
revealed. For the goat ran into a nearby cave, and when
Hayim Elya followed and entered there, the goat led him
through the cave beneath the wall of that orchard, and when
Hayim Elya emerged he found himself inside that garden of
abundance and peace. There he quenched his thirst and
hunger, and there too he learned from a voice in the wind
how it had happened that that goat had been a scapegoat
which had not wanted to be sent to Azazel—so Elijah himself
had been sent to slaughter it, after which he led its soul to *Gan
Eden.* And there it had been serving to lead others inside ever
since. After that Hayim Elya fell asleep with a smile on his
face, and when he awoke, in his own room, Hayim Elya was
still smiling, for now he knew the secret of that white goat.

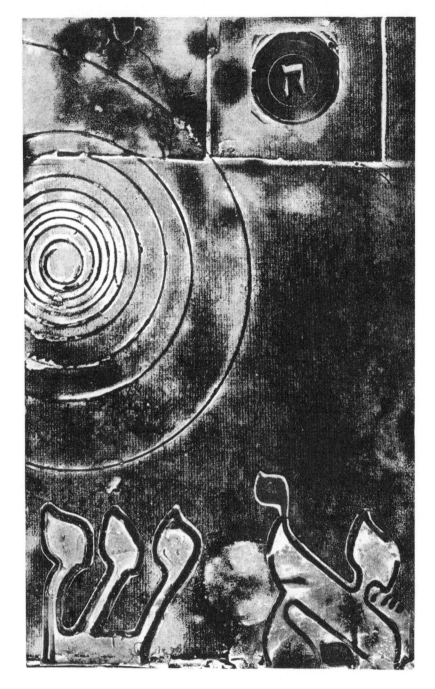

THE TALE OF MALKA NEHAMA

for Edith Altman

I t often happened that petitioners came to see Reb
Zalman not only from Zholkiev, but from the surrounding towns as well. One day a young woman was
brought to see him by her distraught parents. The girl, who
was sixteen, was introduced as Nehamah, but she cried out,
saying: "My name is not Nehamah! It cannot be, since I have
not brought consolation to anyone." And Reb Zalman saw at
once that it was not only the meaning of her name—for
Nehamah means consolation—but the name itself she refused
to accept.

Then her parents told Reb Zalman that they had brought
her to see him not because of her name, by which she refused
to be recognized, but because of another matter, even more
serious. For whenever that young woman set foot inside a
synagogue and heard the prayers being chanted, she began
to shiver almost at once, and if she remained there any longer,
she would faint.

All the time that the parents spoke, Reb Zalman observed Nehamah, and it was quickly apparent that the matter
of the name she refused and her experiences in the

synagogue were linked, although he did not know how. And when her parents had explained the reasons for coming to see him, Reb Zalman turned to Nehamah and said: "Tell me, if you can, what is your true name?" And when Reb Zalman said this, an expression of complete amazement passed over her face, and she said: "Until this very moment I did not know the answer to that. But in the very instant you asked me, I heard the name spoken, as if from someone in this very room." And Reb Zalman said: "And what was the name?" And she replied: "Malka."

Reb Zalman saw that the parents seemed very surprised to hear this name. And he wondered if they might recognize it. When he asked them, the girl's mother replied: "Malka was the name of one of my ancestors, my grandmother's great grandmother. In fact, her full name was Malka Nehamah. My grandmother, Nehamah, was named after her, and my daughter is named after my grandmother, of blessed memory."

Everyone, Malka most of all, was startled to hear this. For although the young woman had known she was named after her grandmother, she did not know that Malka Nehamah was the name of one of her ancestors. And then Reb Zalman said to the mother: "And what was the fate of that Malka Nehamah?" "Oh," sighed the mother, "it was terrible. She lost her life in the Chmielnicki massacres in 1648."

"In what way did she lose her life?" Reb Zalman asked. The mother replied: "She was among two hundred Jews who were crowded into one synagogue in a village near Tultchin, that was set on fire. And she died with all of the others, amid the screams of those flames."

And when the young woman heard this, she collapsed upon the floor and was convulsed with weeping. And Reb Zalman said: "Weep, Malka Nehamah, for that will be your new name. But know as well that the spirit of Malka Nehamah, your ancestor, has come back to this world. Therefore it is time to end the grieving of her old life, which was in another place and time and to be consoled to know that her spirit has returned to this world and time."

And from that day on that young woman was known as Malka Nehamah. And although she was afraid at first when she went back into the synagogue, she soon found that the shivers did not start again, nor did she feel faint. So it was that at last she was able to take part in the prayers and share in their blessings.

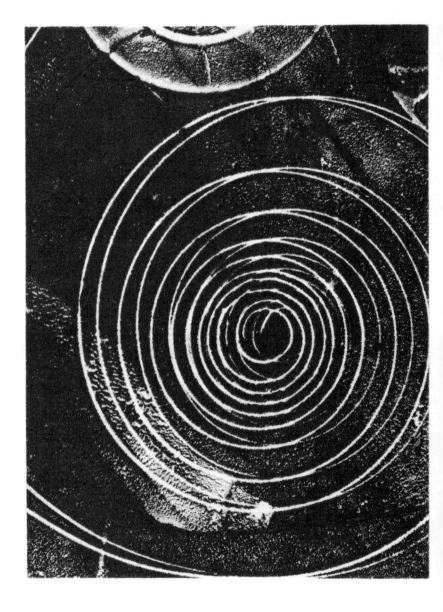

A WANDERING SOUL

for Little Sister Michele Edith

While traveling in the town of Lublin, Reb Hayim Elya heard of a nun whose knowledge of the sources was as great as that of any rabbi. It was said that this nun studied the Scriptures in Hebrew and Aramaic, and that she also spent her time in the study of the Talmud and the *Midrash*. It was also rumored that some of her sister nuns had been heard to say more than once that although she was a nun, she was more of a Jew than a Christian.

Reb Zalman was very distraught when Hayim Elya told him about this nun. And he looked at Hayim Elya and said: "Please go and find her and deliver a letter from me." Then Reb Zalman took up a pen and quill and he wrote something on a page and folded it and sealed it and gave it to Hayim Elya. And he said: "Give this to the nun when you find her."

Now Hayim Elya had not expected this assignment, and he was somewhat reluctant to undertake it. But he reminded himself that the ways of destiny are mysterious, and that sometimes one must undertake a task without knowing its purpose in advance. So Hayim Elya returned to Lublin and found the convent where the nun lived, serving as a teacher. He could not bring himself to go into the convent, and so too would they be alarmed to see a Jew in their midst. So instead he hired a peasant lad to deliver the letter for him, and to wait and see if the nun wished to send back a reply.

This indeed is what happened. The lad brought back a letter from the nun addressed to Reb Zalman, and like the letter that was sent, it too was sealed. And Hayim Elya was very curious to know what Reb Zalman had written, and what was the reply. But he was merely the messenger, and since he could not open the letter, addressed to Reb Zalman, he returned to Zholkiev and delivered the letter to him. Reb Zalman opened it at once, and a look of great pain passed over his face.

Hayim Elya could not bear the mystery any longer, and he begged Reb Zalman to let him know the full story. And Reb Zalman said: "This nun is indeed more of a Jew than a Christian. For when you first told me of her, I saw that this nun bore the soul of a Jew. That night I prayed for her, and the history of her soul was revealed to me. During a pogrom a Jewish infant, whose parents had been slaughtered, had been brought to a convent. She was raised as a Catholic, and she was not told that she was Jewish. This fact was kept secret, and the girl never found out.

"But the soul of that child was one of the pure souls, which hid in the Garden of Eden at the time of the Fall, and thus were untouched by the taint of that sin. And so it was that this soul was forced to go through life with its true destiny as a Jew unfulfilled. Yet even though she was raised in a convent, she was drawn from the first to all things Jewish. And thus it is that she is living out her life in a convent, while surrounding herself with the riches of her true heritage.

"Now when all of this was made clear to me, I wondered how much was known to this nun. Therefore I wrote her the biblical verse in which the first reference to Serach bat Asher is given. *There was also their sister Serach.* For her name appears in the *Tanach* twice: she is listed among those who went into Egypt with Jacob, and among those counted in the census that

Moses took in the wilderness: *The name of Asher's daughter was Serach.* Now the rabbis say that it is the same Serach bat Asher who is being referred to, who remained alive all that time, almost four hundred years. But this would be known only to one who had studied the Midrash. Therefore I sent her that verse, to see how she would respond. For I wondered how much she knew of her own destiny. But I did not want to reveal to her what she did not know. In her letter she returned a message which bore the second reference to Serach in the wilderness. That told that she is aware of the rabbinic inter- pretation, and also that her soul knows of its origin."

Now when Hayim Elya heard this tale, he too despaired, for a light had been denied its true vessel, a light that might have shone brightly in Torah among her own. But something about the history of the soul that Reb Zalman had related bothered him, and Hayim Elya said: "But why was such a pure Jewish soul denied its true destiny?" And Reb Zalman replied: "I was wondering if you would ask me that, Hayim Elya. The reason is that I also saw that this is not the last life of that soul, for the next time that soul comes back it will finally return through the circles of *gilgul* as a Jew. And then, because of the constant yearning of that light for its own vessel, it will invest itself so fully in life as a Jewish woman that the world will be changed by virtue of her presence. For such was the destiny of that pure soul from the first."

THE MATZOS OF
FAITH AND HEALING

O nce, after *Simhas Torah,* a farmer came to Reb Zalman and asked him for a blessing. Reb Zalman replied: "You are a farmer. Everything you do is in God's hands. Do you have faith enough?" And the farmer confessed that he did not. Then Reb Zalman said: "Your faith has become starved. It must be fed. What are you carrying with you in your wagon?" And the farmer replied: "A bag of seeds." And Reb Zalman said: "What grows from those seeds?" And the farmer said: "Winter wheat." And he asked him to describe how wheat is planted. When he did, Reb Zalman said: "So first you throw the seeds away, then they rot in the earth, yet, before long there is much more." Then Reb Zalman said: "Give that bag to me." And the farmer went out to the wagon and gave the bag to Reb Zalman, although he had planned to use it to pay a debt.

Reb Zalman cradled the bag of seeds in his arms, not unlike the way he held the Torah. Then he gave the bag to the man and said: "Plant these seeds in the same place. Cut the wheat that grows from them, grind it, and make *matzos.* Then bring me those *matzos* before *Pesach.* And when you

deliver them to me I will give you the blessing." The farmer
nodded at these words, although he found them strange. And
he did exactly as Reb Zalman had said, planting the seeds,
tending and harvesting them, grinding them into flour and
baking *matzos* with them. And perhaps because he had
planted those seeds in a field apart from the others, the farmer
paid particular attention to the process of their growth. And
he saw how he depended on the Holy One, blessed be He, at
every turn. And in this way his faith was eventually restored.

Then it happened that after he had finished baking the
matzos, which he did by himself, he put them in a bag and set
off in his wagon to deliver them to Reb Zalman. Along the
way he came to a bridge owned by a nobleman, who extracted
a toll from all who crossed there. That day the nobleman
himself was standing there, and when the farmer pulled up
in his wagon, the nobleman asked him what he had in the
sack. (Now if the truth be known, that was not really the
nobleman, but Satan in disguise, who had taken the form of
the Polish nobleman.) The farmer told the nobleman that the
bag contained unleavened bread, without trying to explain
its purpose. Then Satan in disguise said: "Ah, this must be a
miracle. My wife, who is soon expecting a child, has a terrible
craving for unleavened bread, and I had just set out to find it.
Quickly, my good man, give the bag to me."

Now the farmer became very pale when he heard what
the nobleman said, and at first he was very flustered. But then
he grew firm within himself, and he said: "My lord, if the bag
belonged to me, I would not hesitate for an instant in giving
them to you for your wife. But the fact is that the bag belongs
to another, to whom I am but delivering them. And I cannot
give away what does not belong to me."

At this the nobleman seemed to grow angry. Then he
reached into a leather pouch and pulled out a bag, and
opened it so that the farmer could see that it was filled with
gold. He had never seen that much gold in his life. The man
trembled at the sight of it, for there was enough gold there to
make him a wealthy man for the rest of his life. Yet the man
somehow found the strength to resist, and he repeated that

he could not give away what was not his own. (Had he accepted the gold, it would have vanished the first instant he tried to take a piece out of the bag.) Then the nobleman flashed a look of hatred, and reached into the pouch once more, and pulled out another bag of gold, as heavy as the first, and opened it as well, so that the light glinted off the gold coins that filled those bags. Yet the farmer refused to be swayed, handed the nobleman the toll, and took his leave. And as soon as he crossed the bridge, the nobleman vanished, as if he had never been there.

When the farmer reached Reb Zalman's house, Reb Zalman came out to meet him, his face beaming. The farmer took down the bag of *matzos* and handed it to Reb Zalman. Reb Zalman accepted it with gratitude and carried it into his house. What a wonderful *Seder* they had that year! And after *Pesach* Reb Zalman gave the farmer a great blessing, that not only lasted all of his own life, but that of his offspring as well. And as long as he lived, the farmer was never again plagued by the loss of faith that had gnawed at him so long, and the wound of his doubts was healed.

LET IT BE FOR A SIGN

for Rabbi Danny Grossman

Among the Hasidim of Reb Zalman there was one whose name was Reb Dan, who was said to be a descendant of the tribes of Dan. At one time in his life it was believed that Reb Dan was about to lose his hearing. Then he had learned the signs of the deaf, so that he could converse with them. And even though he had recovered, he continued to work with the deaf. His dream was to teach them how to pray in signs.

One day Reb Dan was present as Reb Zalman told the famous tale of the Baal Shem in which many musicians played a music rare and sweet, and all who heard them were caught up in its rhythm, and took up partners and began to dance. Then a deaf man approached there, and when he saw the people swaying and dancing, he thought them madmen. For since he could not hear the music, he could not know the spirit it awakens in its hearers. Likewise did the Baal Shem compare this deaf man to one of the opponents of Hasidism, who came to a Hasidic wedding and was unable to comprehend the revelry he saw there, with musicians playing

and the people dancing joyfully. And when Reb Dan heard
this tale, he cried.

Afterward Reb Zalman told Reb Dan he would like to
talk to him in private. They met together, and Reb Zalman
said: "Why did you cry when I told that tale?" And Reb Dan
said: "It is because I wish to communicate the music of the
Torah to the deaf, so that they can share in its joy." And Reb
Zalman said: "How would you do this?" And Reb Dan said:
"By teaching them how to pray in signs." This surprised Reb
Zalman, for the deaf prayed silently and alone. They did not
daven like the rest. And Reb Zalman mused on this notion,
and at last he said: "Show me, if you please, how you would
say the *Shema* in signs."

Then Reb Dan arose and stood before Reb Zalman. And
Reb Dan made the sign for each one of the first six words of
the Shema. And Reb Zalman, who had never seen these signs
before, recognized the sign for each word. And when Reb
Dan reached the fifth word, *Adonai,* in which God's name is
repeated, Reb Zalman made the sign at the same time as did
Reb Dan. And when Reb Dan saw this he broke into sobs, for
he knew it would be possible to pray by signs after all.

After that Reb Dan assembled a congregation of the deaf,
and taught them how to pray each of the day's services in
signs. And anyone who saw the prayers that congregation
offered up knew for certain that they did in fact hear the
music of the Torah.

That year, on *Yom Kippur,* Reb Zalman discerned the
Holy One had turned a deaf ear to the people. And he
suspected that it had come about because the people had
turned a deaf ear toward the Torah. Then Reb Zalman went
to Reb Dan, and asked him to lead his congregation in the
saying of the *Shema* on *Yom Kippur.* And when the time came
Reb Zalman told the people of the danger confronting
them—that the Holy One had turned a deaf ear. Therefore
he asked them to pray the *Shema* with all their hearts with Reb
Dan, and to make each sign with him as he led them in the
Shema.

And even though the Hasidim of Zholkiev had never heard of such a thing being done, especially on *Yom Kippur*, they did exactly as Reb Zalman had asked, for they trusted him. Thus it was that all of the Hasidim of Zholkiev were transformed into a congregation of the deaf. That first time they prayed the *Shema* in signs the Hasidim made the strange signs as best they could. But when they finished Reb Zalman indicated that they should do it again, and so they did. And then he signaled for them to repeat it. And in this way they went through the signs seven times. And the seventh time every one of them knew those signs as well as the words of the *Shema* that are imprinted on every heart.

And when they had finished that silent *davening,* all of the congregation felt at the same time a sense of great relief. And at that moment Reb Zalman knew that the Holy One was no longer deaf to their prayers, for their prayers were no longer deaf to the Torah.

THE STORYTELLER

In memory of Reuven Gold

There once was a Hasid who was a wonderful
storyteller. It was said that he had begun to tell stories
after hearing tales told by Reb Zalman. About this Reb
Reuven used to say: "I was a baby getting ready to be born.
Reb Zalman was the midwife." At first he did not think of
himself as a storyteller, merely as one who told stories. Little
by little people began to seek him out to hear his tales. They
invited him to dinner just to hear the tales he would tell
afterward. And eventually the day came when he gave up his
daily work and set out into the world as a storyteller.

The name of this storyteller was Reb Reuven ben
Shimon. Except when he was telling tales, he was the shyest
of men, who even stuttered when he spoke. But when he
began to tell a tale, the shyness and the stuttering disappeared. Each word he spoke was a rope that drew the listener
into another world, the world of the tale. And it was said that
none who entered that world left it unchanged.

Now if the truth be known, Reb Reuven did not tell a
great many tales. While some storytellers had as many tales
to tell as there are drops in the ocean or sand on the shore,

Reb Reuven only told a few tales. When asked about this, he always explained that he only told tales that made his heart dance. And anyone who heard him tell a tale could well understand this, for Reb Reuven became as entranced in the tale as any listener hearing it for the first time. And more often than not the tale would move him to tears and joyous laughter.

Once it happened that Reb Reuven told the tale of young Mordecai who was brought to the Rabbi of Karlin because no matter what his parents did, they could not bring him to take his studies seriously. The rabbi bellowed that he would teach the child to study, and had the parents leave the terrified child with him. But as soon as they departed, the rabbi embraced the child, holding him gently to his heart for the longest time, silently. When the parents returned, the rabbi again bellowed that the boy had been taught his lesson. That child grew up to be a wise and compassionate teacher of the Torah, and many was the time he said that he had first learned how to teach Torah when the rabbi had held him to his breast.

Now there was a young woman who heard this tale and was deeply moved by it, and she made the strange request that Reb Reuven tell it once again. While many a storyteller might have refused that request, Reb Reuven did not. Instead he told the story over again, almost word for word as he had the first time. And yet all of those who had heard the first telling could not dispute that while the words had been the same, the story was completely different. How was this possible?

Reb Hayim Elya asked Reb Zalman about this paradox, and added: "And this, Rebbe, is strangest of all: the first time I heard this story it was as if I was held in the embrace of my father. But the second time I heard Reb Reuven as if he were speaking with the voice of my mother." Reb Zalman said: "For Reb Reuven the words are like the notes by which music is read. They serve only as guideposts and not as an end in themselves. And the request to repeat the tale opened Reb Reuven to a new music by which the tale could be told. Just as we chant the Torah in Major and the Prophets in Minor, so too did the ears of the young woman open the mouth of Reb Reuven, for, as Reb Avraham Yitzhak ha-Cohen said, 'There are ears that have the power to open mouths.' For Reb Reuven always comes back to the symphony of the tale as if for the first time and rediscovers its music anew. It is the spirit that stands behind the words which concerns him, and not the words themselves."

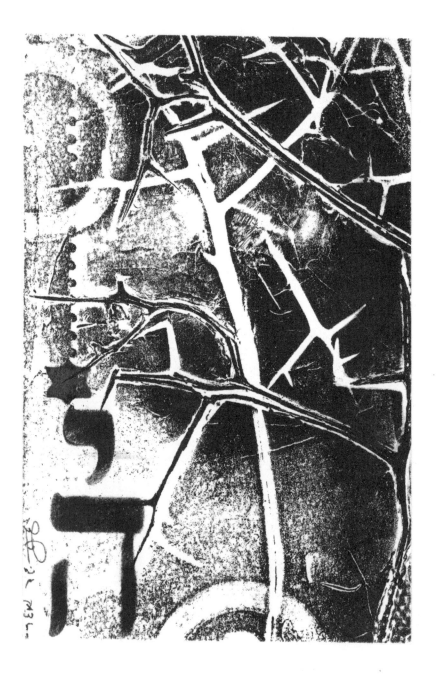

The Man
who was Always Late

Try as he might, Reb Dovid found it impossible to be
on time. It always happened that he either overslept
or became sidetracked and forgot about his meetings. At last
Reb Dovid came to Reb Zalman about it. Reb Zalman was
very curious to know why Reb Dovid was unable to overcome this flaw, so he sent up a dream question about it, and
that night he learned in a dream that Reb Dovid's soul had
always known this affliction. In fact, in a previous life he had
even come late to his place at Mount Sinai. For when the Holy
One had apportioned time to souls, a playful angel had taken
a hundred and one minutes from him and given them to
another soul, one that always arrived too early.

So it was that in subsequent lives, despite all efforts to
correct this flaw, Reb Dovid's soul had continued to suffer
from it. In some lives he had served as a soldier, who had been
punished for not being able to follow orders on time. In other
lives, when he had been a woman, he had missed the time to
light the candles and as a result had desecrated the Sabbath.
Thus when Reb Zalman awoke and recalled this dream, he
recognized that Reb Dovid's flaw, which had haunted him
since the time of the creation of his soul, would not be a simple
one to eliminate. And Reb Zalman gave the matter much

thought, but he could not think of a way to restore to Reb Dovid's soul the hundred and one minutes of which he had been robbed.

Reb Zalman continued to meditate on this matter, and meanwhile Reb Dovid suffered from his flaw, saying his prayers late, after the stars had appeared, and having his *matzos* condemned because they reached the oven too late. These failings caused Reb Dovid great pain, for they were completely unintentional. And the scoldings he got did not help, because of his soul's disposition to tardiness.

The next time Reb Dovid came to Reb Zalman with this problem, Reb Zalman told him that he could not help him in any direct way, and Reb Dovid was so distraught that he forgot to give Reb Zalman a message from Reb Levi of Ludmir, inviting Reb Zalman to serve as the *mohel* at the *bris* of his newborn son. Only once he was on his way did Reb Dovid remember this message. Then he pleaded with the coachman to turn back, and after he promised to pay additional fare the coach did return to Zholkiev. Once again Reb Dovid stood before Reb Zalman in tears, and shrugged his shoulders as if to say, "I'm afraid I have done it again." Then it was difficult for Reb Zalman to arrange things to leave with Reb Dovid at once, so Reb Zalman gave him the bag of the tools for the *bris* and told him to meet him at the home of Reb Levi in the morning. Then Reb Dovid assured Reb Zalman that he would let Reb Levi know that he was coming, and would have everything there on time the next day.

Reb Zalman took the coach early the next morning after *Shaharis,* and hurried to Ludmir. But when he arrived he was not met by Reb Levi or someone from his household as he had expected. At last, with the aid of some children, Reb Zalman found his way to Reb Levi's house, where he saw the strained patience on the faces of those present, but no Reb Dovid with the bag of instruments for the circumcision. This time Reb Zalman too felt anger at Reb Dovid rising in him, and he explained that he could not go on with the *bris* until Reb Dovid arrived.

Then someone left to fetch Reb Dovid and found him asleep. He woke him, got Reb Zalman's bag, and asked Reb Dovid to hurry for he too was needed for the *bris*. Meanwhile, at Reb Levi's house, they began making preparations for the *bris*. The table was set and Reb Zalman began a chant to invite Elijah to join them. Suddenly Reb Dovid entered and the air was charged, and Reb Zalman realized that it was not right to proceed with the *bris* while so much anger was in the air. So he turned to Reb Dovid and said: "Before we can complete the covenant of the *bris*, we must remove the taint of anger that hangs in the air, so that it will not cling to the moment of the child's covenant. Therefore I must ask you to lie face down on the circumcision table." Reb Dovid and the others were amazed at these words, but Reb Dovid did not resist, and did as Reb Zalman had said.

Then Reb Zalman turned to the others present and said: "Let those who felt anger toward Reb Dovid, as I did, come forward and place your hands on his back. Instead of scolding him we will put the power of our anger at the disposal of his soul. For does he himself not scold himself enough as it is? For know that his soul is innocent of this failing, and longs to be on time. What is needed is that each of us give his soul a few minutes of our lives, so that it may have restored to it the time that was snatched away so long ago."

And although the others present did not understand what Reb Zalman meant, still each and every one came forward and placed their hands on Reb Dovid's back, and in this way each of them gave him a few moments of their lives. And Reb Dovid wept without ceasing, for in all his lives he had not been met with so much love. And after that Reb Dovid no longer had a problem with time, but arrived promptly everywhere, and became known as one who could be fully depended upon. As for the child, the love and warmth present at the time of his *bris* made the seal of the blessing of the covenant so strong that it could never be broken, and his love and loyalty to his heritage and to the Holy One Himself, blessed be He, never wavered.

THE TALE OF THE MENORAH

One year it happened that the *Yahrtzeit* of Reb Nachman of Bratslav fell on the Sabbath, and after a fine *Shabbas* meal and the singing of many songs, Reb Zalman of Zholkiev repeated to those present Reb Nachman's tale of the menorah. And this is the tale as Reb Zalman told it that night: "Once a young man left his home and traveled for several years. Afterward, when he returned home, he proudly told his father that he had become a master of making menorahs. He asked his father to call together all those who practiced this craft in that town, that he might demonstrate his unrivaled skill for them.

"That is what his father did, inviting them to their home. But when his son showed them the menorah he had made, not everyone found it pleasing in their sight. Then his father went to each and every one and begged them to tell him the truth about what they thought of it. And at last each one admitted that he had found a defect in the menorah.

"When the father reported this to his son, the young man asked to know what was the defect they had found, and it emerged that each of the guests had noted something different. What one craftsman had praised, another had found defective; nor did they agree on what was the defect in that menorah, and what was the most beautiful aspect of it.

"And the son said to his father: 'By this have I shown my great skill. For I have revealed to each one his own defect, since each of these defects was actually in he who perceived it. It was these defects that I incorporated into my creation, for I made this menorah only from defects. Now I will begin its restoration.'"

When Reb Zalman had retold this tale, he saw it was still taking root in the souls of his Hasidim. And he said: "I see that Reb Nachman's words still echo in this world, as well they should, since he brought them to us from on high. Since this night is his *Yahrtzeit*, let all of us open ourselves to his spirit, which is surely present among us, and let us ask him if we might inquire further into the mystery of the menorah of defects." And no sooner had Reb Zalman said this, than each of his Hasidim discovered he could express his deepest understanding of Reb Nachman's tale.

Then Reb Zalman turned to Hayim Elya, his scribe, and bade him speak. And Hayim Elya said: "Surely this *maaseh* of Reb Nachman's illustrates a secret about the process of *tikkun*, of restoration and redemption. The purpose of that menorah, then, was to make the others aware of their defects, for only when this awareness has been attained can the process of *tikkun* begin."

Reb Zalman and the other Hasidim were pleased with this interpretation, and marvelled at the skill of the craftsman who could capture the essence of another's defects. Then Reb Zalman turned to Reb Simcha, and bid him to speak. And Reb Simcha said: "Surely the menorah represents the way a *Tzaddik* may serve his Hasidim—as a mirror to make them aware of their defects, so that they may initiate the process of *tikkun*, as it is written in the Talmud: 'Anyone who finds a flaw finds his own flaw." And this interpretation was also pleasing to the Hasidim, for it applied to Reb Zalman above all, who had served as a mirror in which they had been able to recognize their destiny, as well as their defects.

After this Reb Zalman turned to Reb Sholem, and asked him to reveal his understanding of the tale. And Reb Sholem said: "Surely the model for that menorah existed before the creation of the world. Then each branch of it was a perfect vessel, unbroken and complete. But in order for creation to take place it was required that these vessels be broken, so that they could spill their sparks of light into the world. This is what we refer to as the Shattering of the Vessels. Thus the branches of that menorah were broken vessels, and that is why they appeared defective to the others. For it was necessary for them to first recognize that the vessels had been broken before they could begin their restoration." And when the others had heard Reb Sholem's commentary, they felt that it also rang true.

Then Reb Zalman turned to Reb Avraham ben Yitzhak, who was also present that night, and bade him make known the meaning of the tale as he understood it. And Reb Avraham said: "Surely the craftsman who created this menorah is none other than the Holy One, blessed be He. Therefore the seven branches of the menorah represent the seven days of creation, and the light of the flames of the menorah represents the primordial light, which came into existence on the first day of creation, when God said *Let there be light, and there was light,* while the menorah itself is this world. And why is it a menorah of defects? Because the defects are the defects of this world, since *God formed man out of the dust of the earth.*" And the others marveled at these words, and understood how the tale might also be an allegory of the creation of the world.

Now the last of Reb Zalman's Hasidim who had not yet spoken was Reb Naftali, who was steeped in the mysteries of the Kabbalah. And when Reb Zalman turned to him, Reb Naftali said: "Surely the seven branches of the menorah represent the seven *Sefirot* that emanate in the world below, while the oil, the wick and the flame of the branches represent the three *Sefirot* of the world above. And thus the menorah reveals how the worlds above and below may be drawn together, so that the light originating in the world above may also be reflected here below. That such a menorah would appear defective in the eyes of men is not surprising, for when the light of the *Shekhinah* is withdrawn, this world has no more substance than a shadow. But when the light of the *Shekhinah* illuminates our vision, we will be able to perceive it from the perspective of the world above, where its perfection cannot be denied." And the words of Reb Naftali illuminated the understanding of everyone who heard them, and they began to recognize that the waters of meaning ran far deeper than they had first realized.

It was then that Reb Zalman spoke for the first time, and he said: "Surely this menorah can be likened to an opal. An opal's most distinguishing feature is the fire of its center, but this fire is also its flaw. When seen from one angle, the fire resembles nothing more than a crack, but from another perspective it is the most beautiful part. Thus what appears to some to be a defect in the menorah is what makes it unique and more beautiful.

"Now consider that the menorah in Reb Nachman's *maaseh* was actually *perfect* in every respect, and it was only the vision of those who beheld it that was flawed. When the *tikkun* had at last taken place and their eyes were opened, they saw that menorah in all its splendor, with each branch representing one of the seven heavens, which opened up before their eyes." And with these words each of those present was uplifted on one of the branches of that menorah into the celestial Paradise, and when they looked down from the heights they saw that the seven flames of the menorah all burned as a single flame, and that flame illuminated the Bearer of every blessing. And there they also saw the spirit of Reb Nachman, which had been present among them all along, and all understood that he was the one who had provided the clarity of their perceptions. And at that moment they heard Reb Nachman's voice echo in their souls, saying: "Surely all that you have said about that menorah is true, for it is like an immense, many-faceted jewel, and each of you has turned to gaze at a new facet, for the facets of the jewel are infinite. Yet it is but a single jewel you see, eternal and unchanging. And that is the jewel in the crown of the King of Kings, who is none other than the craftsman who constructed this menorah so that the flames burning below might ascend on high, and all the world could be illumined by their light."

REB NACHMAN'S SPIRIT

for Arthur and Kathy Green

T hree Bratslav Hasidim, who had traveled to the Holy Land from various parts of the world, gathered in Jerusalem in the home of Reb Gedaliah, who had tailored his soul to the teachings of Reb Nachman. There they wasted no time, but began at once to speak of the mystery and blessing of the Rebbe who, while no longer among the living, still guided their lives with his powerful presence.

Reb Aryeh was the first to speak, and he said: "When a man dies, his soul remains linked to this world for eleven months, then ascends into the upper realms, where it is remote from the concerns of men. But there are those souls that for one reason or another remain among the living, and make their presence known there. Such is the spirit of Reb Nachman, roving from rung to rung, whose presence in this world after his death is even more powerful than was his living presence, which itself shone like a bright flame at midnight."

Then Reb Gedaliah, the oldest of the four, spoke and
said: "I have often wondered why it is that our Rebbe's spirit
chose to renounce the eternal rewards of Paradise, which he
had so richly earned, and instead seeks out in every generation those who are destined to be his Hasidim. For as we
know, on his deathbed Reb Nachman instructed his Hasidim
not to appoint another in his place, as is the custom, since he
would remain their Rebbe even after his death. And we have
honored his wish, and just as we have continued to seek his
guidance in his teachings and tales, so has his soaring spirit
continued to seek us out in dreams and even while waking
to instruct us further in the secrets by which a kingdom can
be made to flourish. Many are the accounts of those who have
encountered Reb Nachman's spirit and been enriched im-
measurably as a result. For his spirit is held back by no
boundaries, and reaches out to those the world over whose
souls have an affinity to his pure *neshamah*."

Then Reb Avraham Yitzhak, who had traveled the furthest to be there that day, spoke and said: "In every generation there are those who are destined to be the Hasidim of
Reb Nachman. And some of these are those who serve in
synagogues in Jerusalem and Safed and other cities, and
identify themselves to the world as Bratslaver Hasidim, as we
do. But there are also others, bearers of the fragments of the
broken tablets, who go their separate ways, and conceal their
true loyalty from the world, and serve the Rebbe in secret.
And, strange as it may seem, Reb Nachman loves these hidden Hasidim even more than those who serve him openly,
for those who remain hidden maintain an inward vision that
permits them to contemplate the light of the kingdom at all
times."

To this Reb Zalman replied: "The tales of the encounters
of Reb Nachman's spirit with his Hasidim, both the hidden
and revealed, are myriad. One will no more than open the
volume of Reb Nachman's tales and read one word when this
spirit will reach out to him and transmit in full one of the
untold tales that the Rebbe took with him into the afterlife,
which in his beneficence he still sees fit to bestow on the

world of men. And even without fully understanding how such a miracle could occur, the Hasid will carefully record the secret he has been blessed to receive and transmit, and give thanks that the Rebbe saw fit to let him serve as his vessel. Yet another will receive one part of an untold tale in one dream, and the conclusion in another, so carefully does the Rebbe's spirit reveal these mysteries so that nothing will be lost in the transmission, and the tale may be told in full. Still another will suddenly hear the voice of the Rebbe speaking to him from the Other World, and like the Rebbe's loyal scribe, Reb Nussan, will hurry to record all that is revealed, never questioning the miracle by which the Rebbe's spirit has reached out to him."

Then Reb Gedaliah returned to his original question and said: "Still unanswered is the mystery of why the Rebbe's spirit sees fit to remain in such close contact with the living, rather than join the souls of the righteous in Paradise. Also unanswered is whether this contact should be regarded as a reward or punishment for the Rebbe's spirit, since it is impossible to imagine that anyone would renounce the rewards of Paradise to serve as a messenger among men. After all, for the single sin of striking the rock with his staff rather than speaking to it as the Holy One had commanded, Moses was denied entrance into the Holy Land. So too must we consider the possibility that the fate of Reb Nachman's spirit to wander, beneficial as it is to all of us, may constitute some kind of punishment. But for what could it be, since the life of the Rebbe was without blemish?"

To this Reb Avraham Yitzkak replied: "No, there is one sin in the eyes of Heaven for which the Rebbe must be held accountable, although he appears blameless in our eyes. And this is the same sin from which the Baal Shem could not withhold himself—that of seeking to force the Messiah to descend from the Bird's Nest where he awaits the ram's horn that will announce his arrival, and of hastening the End of Days. If the blessing of Reb Nachman's spirit in remaining among us is a form of repentance, it is surely for his using his great resources during his lifetime in seeking to hasten the End."

Reb Aryeh quickly replied, saying: "In this you are wrong, Reb Avraham Yitzhak, for of all sins there is none towards which Heaven shows more mercy than that of seeking to hasten the coming of the Messiah. But in any case the blessing of the presence of Reb Nachman's abundant spirit among us is not a punishment, but a reward. Consider that during Reb Nachman's lifetime he consistently denied himself the pleasures of the living, and focused his thoughts at all times on the true mysteries. Thus, because he concentrated so intently on the other world while living among men, he was rewarded after his death by being permitted to return to this world. Here he serves as the flame that illumines the true meaning of the Torah, and what greater reward could there be?"

Reb Zalman nodded at these words and said: "Yes, because Reb Nachman sought all his life to make the world ready to receive the Messiah—may He come in our time!—he has been rewarded in the afterlife by being permitted to continue this work of gathering the sparks and restoring the vessels, so that the Messianic days may come that much sooner."

Reb Avraham Yitzkak smiled when he heard these words and said: "You are right of course, Reb Zalman. The truth is that Reb Nachman was the *Tzaddik* of his generation, and had the time been right he would have been revealed to the world as no less than Messiah ben Joseph, he who prepares the way for Messiah ben David, who in turn will bring the End of Days. But because the conditions were not right during Reb Nachman's lifetime, he has been permitted to continue to make the world ready to receive the Messiah after his death."

To this Reb Gedaliah added: "Let us be grateful that a soul such as Reb Nachman's was permitted to descend from the Tree of Souls in the first place, and that our Rebbe's wish to remain among us even in the afterlife has been granted. For this reveals that the Holy One not only recognizes the longing of his children for the coming of the Messiah, but the longing of the Messiah himself to be present among us. And to make his presence possible that much sooner, the Holy One, Blessed be He, has permitted the spirit of Reb Nachman to remain among us to perform the acts of *tikkun* that will ultimately make it possible for the Messiah to come. For this there is much to give thanks!"

Reb Zalman
Becomes a Beggar

Once, while Reb Zalman was in the Holy Land, he was praying at the *Kotel,* the Wailing Wall. His prayers that day were for those he loved who were unmarried, and he prayed that their *Shidduch* might take place. Suddenly a beggar came up to him and held out his hand before him and said "*Tzedekah, Tzedekah!*" Reb Zalman turned to him and said: "What is it for?" And the beggar replied: "For the dowry of a bride." And when Reb Zalman heard this, he reached in his pocket and gave the beggar all the money he had. For that beggar might well have been Elijah, and the dowry he collected intended for those for whom Reb Zalman had been praying.

After the beggar had departed, however, Reb Zalman realized that he no longer had enough money to live on that day, and he was far from where he was staying, too far to walk. Yet he did not even have the money to hire a carriage to take him home. And Reb Zalman suddenly realized that he had become a beggar. Then he left the *Kotel* and walked into the Old City and went into a store. And he asked the owner to give him enough to hire a carriage. The store owner, who was a Jew, offered to give him the money as a loan. But Reb Zalman replied: "No, I want you to give it to me outright, for today I am a beggar. And as any beggar will tell you, the *mitzvah* of *Tzedekah* cannot be fulfilled with a loan. That is why God created beggars—so that others might be able to fulfill that *mitzvah*." And when the store keeper heard this, he gave Reb Zalman the money he needed, and Reb Zalman thanked him and blessed him in return.

And all that day Reb Zalman was a happy man, who had managed to be a beggar in Jerusalem after having emptied his pockets to help endower a bride. For in this way the Holy One, blessed be He, had permitted him both to give and to receive, and all on the same day.

THE TALE OF THE MEZZUZAH

for Gerd, Sarah and Avraham Stern

While in the holy city of Jerusalem, Reb Zalman came into possession of several old manuscripts, including one said to have been copied by a son of Rabbi Hayim Vital, the primary disciple of the Ari, Rabbi Isaac Luria. The son, himself a *sopher,* had copied out ten copies of his father's book *Etz Hayim,* one for each of the ten *Sefirot.* And that book which Reb Zalman came to possess was the ninth of those ten copies.

Now when Reb Zalman opened that book, something fell out from between the pages. Reb Zalman saw that it was a parchment, and when he looked at it he saw that the *Shema* was inscribed there, and he realized that it was the parchment of a *Mezzuzah.* And that parchment was very old, even older than the manuscript in which it had been hidden. And Reb Zalman studied that parchment and saw that it had been inscribed without a single flaw, and therefore could serve in a *Mezzuzah.* Therefore, when Reb Zalman returned to Zholkiev, he placed that parchment inside the *Mezzuzah* which guarded the front door of his home. And from the first

Reb Zalman noticed that a new spirit of peace was present in his home, and everyone who lived there shared in it.

Then it happened that one morning, as Reb Zalman kissed the *Mezzuzah* on his way out of the house, that he heard a voice nearby that whispered: *"Shema Yisrael,"* Hear, O Israel. Reb Zalman was startled, and looked around to see who was there, but he saw no one. And because those were the first words of the *Shema,* which is inscribed inside the parchment of every *Mezzuzah,* Reb Zalman looked at the *Mezzuzah,* and just then he heard the words *"Adonai Elohenu, Adonai Ahad,"* the Lord our God, the Lord is One. And those whispered words came directly from the *Mezzuzah.* And suddenly Reb Zalman understood that the parchment he had found inside the manuscript of *Etz Hayim* had a voice of its own, which had spoken. And Reb Zalman was staggered, for if that were true, the *Mezzuzah* could serve him as an oracle, from which he might discern the Way of the Righteous.

Then Reb Zalman meditated on those six words of the *Shema.* And even though he had thought of them over and over all his life, and had spoken them several times each day, always with *kavannah,* Reb Zalman had a new insight into them. For now he heard them in two parts, first, "Hear, O Israel," which seemed like a message in itself, announcing that he should listen; then, "the Lord our God, the Lord is One," which he heard as if spoken by the Holy One Himself, as if He were calling out to him. And Reb Zalman knew that he had been greatly blessed.

So it was that after that, whenever a decision of great importance had to be made, Reb Zalman would stand before the *Mezzuzah* and he would hear one of the words, or a phrase, of the *Shema* spoken, in that same whispered voice. And when he did, he would meditate on those words, such as "liest down" or "riseth up." And when he did, he saw how they spoke directly to him of his life, and guided him on the right path.

In fact, Reb Zalman was guided in this way in the decision to permit Reb Hayim Elya to serve as his *sopher* and write his tales down. For when he brought this question with him, he heard the whispered voice say "write them," from the phrase "write them on the doorposts of thy house, and upon thy gates." And then he knew that the tales must be written down.

On one occasion Reb Zalman was leaving home to set out on a journey by ship. But when he stood before the *Mezzuzah* he heard the words "sittest in thine house," and he turned around and did not go. And it happened that a terrible storm arose while that ship was at sea, and it was driven off course and crashed against the rocks, and everyone on it lost their lives. After that, Reb Zalman always consulted the *Mezzuzah*, and its words, consisting of phrases drawn from the *Shema*, never failed to reveal the true path.

On another occasion the Jewish community of Zholkiev was in danger of a pogrom. A dangerous priest was inciting the people against them, accusing the Jews of not loving the Emperor and even repeating the blood-libel. The rabbis of Zholkiev met together, and all recognized that with the approach of *Pesach* there was the real danger of the Jews being accused of the blood-libel. As in the past, a Christian child would be killed, and its body hidden in the Jewish ghetto. And when it would be found, the people would be incited to riot against the Jews. This had happened time and time again. In the days of Rabbi Loew, he had created a golem, a man of clay, and brought him to life with the magic of the Name. But in the days of Reb Zalman there were no more golems to be found, for there was none among them who knew the secret permutation of the Name.

The rabbis agreed that one of them must go and see the Emperor, to assure him that they were loyal citizens, so that the pogrom could be forestalled. It was Reb Zalman who was chosen to go. At first he was filled with fear, for he did not know what he might say that would cause the Emperor to trust him and offer his protection to the Jews. And for two days he sat in his room alone, and did not come out. Then, on the third day, he stood before the *Mezzuzah*, seeking guidance, and he heard a voice whisper the words "walkest by the way." And then he knew that it was destined that he go, and he lost his fear.

But he still did not know what he should do when he reached the Emperor. Then, all at once, he heard the whispered voice emerge from the *Mezzuzah*, which said "And thou shalt bind them for a sign upon thine hand, and they shall be for frontlets between thine eyes." And Reb Zalman knew that the solution somehow involved his *tefillin*, and he packed the *tallis*-coat he had received from Reb Sholem, and the *teffilin* he had received in Tismenitz, and set off for the capital to meet with the Emperor.

When Reb Zalman came into the capital, he found that the people all seemed downcast, and even the eyes of the Jews were filled with tears. Reb Zalman asked a passerby what was wrong, and thus he learned that the Emperor's daughter had a large abscess in her throat and was very ill. Reb Zalman was very sorry to hear this, not only because it grieved him to learn that anyone suffered, but also since the Emperor would surely refuse to see him at that time, which posed such great danger for the Jews.

Then it occurred to him that he might go to the Emperor and offer the prayers and blessings of the Jews. But when he reached the palace, the guards refused to permit him an audience. Turned back, Reb Zalman asked to be told where the bedroom of the princess was to be found, and he was shown the window of her room. Then he stood there, beneath the window, and took out his *tallis*-coat and *tefillin* and put them on and began to pray outside her window.

Now it happened that at that very moment the princess was looking down from that window, for she was tired of having been in that same room for so many days. And thus it was that she saw Reb Zalman as he prayed beneath her window, and when she saw how strange he looked with his *tallis*-coat and *tefillin*—for she had never seen them worn before—she broke out into laughter. And she laughed so hard that she broke the abscess in her throat, and thus she was relieved of that terrible pain and soon recovered. And when the Emperor heard that this miracle had come about because she had laughed, he asked to know what it was that she was laughing about. And when she told him it was because of the strange appearance of the Jew praying outside her window, the Emperor commanded that the Jew be brought to him.

So it was that Reb Zalman found himself in the presence of the Emperor, and thus had the occasion, for the first time in his life, to pronounce the blessing our sages decreed be said in the presence of a sovereign. So too did he offer a blessing of thanksgiving over the recovery of the princess. And after this the Emperor told him that because of the good luck he had brought them he could have any wish of his choice. Reb Zalman reminded his Imperial Majesty that healing, peace and prosperity come from laughter, but that laughter is inhibited by fear. And it was then that Reb Zalman told the Emperor of the dangers facing the Jews of Zholkiev, and the Emperor did not hesitate, but wrote a decree giving the Jews of the city his personal protection, and he sent a troop of guards with Reb Zalman, which he stationed in the city from that time on. And the only purpose of that troop was to see that no danger threatened the Jews of that city, whose lives had been protected so well by the hints of the Holy One that were made known to Reb Zalman through the words of the *Shema* as the voice whispered them from that magic *Mezzuzah*.

THE TALE OF THE OLIVE OIL

O nce a *melamed* came to Reb Zalman and confessed
that he felt he must have committed a sin, although
he wasn't sure what it was. For he had looked back at all of
the children he had taught and many of them had not followed the path of the righteous. And he wondered if there
was anything about his teaching that had led them astray.
Therefore he had asked Reb Chazkel ben Meir to sit in the
back of his class. And after the class Reb Chazkel had told him
that his teaching was too solemn; it failed to convey the joy
of the study of the Torah. All it conveyed was the letter of the
Law. And now the teacher, recognizing the truth of Reb
Chazkel's words, had come to Reb Zalman to seek a way of
doing *teshuvah,* repentance.

Reb Zalman listened closely to what the *melamed* said,
and then he replied, saying: "You have been teaching for so
many years that the joy has somehow gone out of it. Therefore I would send you to the Holy Land, for if the joy of the
Torah can be found anywhere, it is in the Land. So it is that I
am sending you on a mission: I want you to bring back a bottle

of olive oil for me to use to light the menorah next Hanukah. And I want you to make that olive oil yourself."

Now Hanukah had just passed that year, and the *melamed* understood that Reb Zalman was giving him one year to go to the Holy Land and come back and bring with him that olive oil. And he accepted this form of *teshuvah* and set out as soon as possible for the Holy Land. And everything worked out smoothly, so that he arrived in the port of Jaffa in *Eretz Yisrael* four months later. Then he knew he had four months in which to come to know the land, and to learn, as well, how to make olive oil.

But the *melamed* found, to his distress, that everyone he asked about how to make olive oil laughed at him, saying "Why don't you just buy olive oil? It's already made." Every time he asked about this he got a similar reaction, and the four months he spent in the Holy Land passed quickly, until he realized that it was almost time to return to Poland and he still had not learned how to make olive oil. So one night when he sat down in his room by himself, with a basket full of olives, he took an olive in his hand and recalled the name of one of the children that he had taught. Then he took two stones and pressed that olive between them with all his strength, and let its juice run into a tray. And he said to himself, "Oy, what have I done to his *neshamah*. Every time he had some joy I squeezed it out of him."

Then he continued, olive by olive, to recall the students in all the classes he had taught. And each time he squeezed the olive between two stones until its juice ran into the tray, where it mixed with his tears. And so it went until midnight, when he had recalled the name of each and every student. Then he poured the olive oil from that tray into a jug and, dispirited and in a state of complete exhaustion, he fell asleep.

While he was asleep the *melamed* dreamed that one of these children came to him and said: "The remorse you felt as you squeezed the olives made me want to forgive you." And while the *melamed* continued to sleep, each and every soul of every student he had ever taught flocked before him, and each and every one gave him his forgiveness. And when he awoke in the morning, the *melamed* felt that a great yoke had been lifted from him, and that day, for the first time, he sensed the sacredness of the Holy Land and appreciated it.

On his return to Zholkiev, the *melamed* came to see Reb Zalman and handed him the small jug of olive oil that he had pressed with his own hands. He was ashamed that there was so little oil to be found there—not more than could be expected to burn for one night—but when he told Reb Zalman the tale of how he had made it, Reb Zalman told him not to worry. And when the time came to burn that oil in the *Hanukiah*, the ancient miracle occurred again, and the oil that was not enough for more than one night lasted eight nights. And thus heaven made it known that the *teshuvah* of the *melamed* had truly been accepted on high, and that the souls of his students had truly forgiven him.

THE SECRET OF THE MENORAH

for Sarina and Bernie Berlow

Now it was a custom of Reb Zalman to light two menorahs on *Hanukah,* one in the window downstairs facing East, and the other in the window upstairs, also facing East. First he would say the blessing and light the menorah downstairs, and then he would repeat the blessing in a whisper and light the menorah upstairs. His Hasidim regarded this *minhag* as strange, and even stranger was the fact that Reb Zalman would put more oil in the menorah upstairs than that downstairs. And for hours after the menorah downstairs had burned out, Reb Zalman would sit before the candles of the menorah upstairs and stare into the flames.

On several occasions his Hasidim asked him about this practice, but Reb Zalman refused to reveal the reason for it, or even to say why he sat so long in front of the candles. This had the effect of making the Hasidim even more curious, and they began to speculate among themselves. Reb Shmuel Leib said that Reb Zalman might have identified the menorah downstairs with the body, while the menorah upstairs represented the soul, and that he spent hours peering into those flames because he had always been one to seek out the secrets of the soul. Reb Dovid thought that the menorah downstairs represented this world, while the menorah upstairs represented the world to come. Reb Feivel the Dark agreed with this interpretation, and added to it that Reb Zalman no doubt put more oil in the upstairs lamp because our souls will exist long after our bodies have returned to dust. But Reb Feivel the White disagreed with all of these interpretations, and said that Reb Zalman probably had learned the custom from his father, and did it even though he did not know the reason for it, as a way of honoring his father's memory.

Reb Hayim Elya listened to these speculations, and they all seemed reasonable to him, but he wanted to know if any of them were correct, and if so, which one. Therefore, on the last night of *Hanukah* that year, Hayim Elya sat down next to Reb Zalman as he peered into the flames of the menorah upstairs, and he too observed the shapes of the flames as they burned. Reb Zalman did not acknowledge Hayim Elya, but neither did he seem to mind his presence, and he simply continued to stare into the flames. So Hayim Elya remained there and did the same.

Now for the first hour Hayim Elya was completely mystified as to what the Rebbe might find so fascinating in those flames, but he kept his eyes fixed on them in any case. Then, an hour or so later, a strange thing occurred. Hayim Elya found himself thinking about his own departed father, Reb Nussan. He did not know what prompted these thoughts, but they were very intense indeed, and before long Hayim Elya began to weep. The tears caused his eyes to become blurred, and when he looked at the flames of the candles it seemed to him that he could almost see his father's face peering out of one of the flames, that of the *Shammash*. This was curious indeed, and Hayim Elya peered closer, expecting the mirage to vanish. But it did not; he saw his father's face there more clearly than ever.

Soon afterward Hayim Elya found himself thinking about his father's father, Reb Yehezkel, also departed from this life. And lo and behold, as he stared into the flames he could have sworn that he saw the face of Reb Yehezkel there in the flame of one candle, that of the first night. Now when this happened Hayim Elya suddenly felt a chill run down his spine, and he stared rapidly in succession at each of the remaining candles, and in each and every one of them he saw the face of another departed soul to whom he had been close in this life: the face of Leah, wife of Reb Yehezkel, Hayim Elya's grandmother on his father's side; the face of his mother's father, Reb Zev; the face of Reb Zev's wife, Raizel, Hayim Elya's grandmother on his mother's side; the face of Reb Yehudah, the *sopher* who had taught him how to write a *Sefer Torah;* the face of Anath, a girl that Hayim Elya had loved as a boy, who had drowned in a tragic accident; the face of Reb Benjamin, who had often told wonderful tales to Hayim Elya as a child, and who had instilled in him a great love for the *Aggadah;* and he saw one other face, which he had never seen before in his life, yet he recognized that face at once: it was the face of Reb Nachman of Bratslav, whose wandering spirit in the world, he now saw with certainty, watched over him as well.

Now when Hayim Elya saw how he was surrounded with these beloved spirits, and how they all were present before him at the same time, he was completely overwhelmed, and broke into tears of joy mixed with sorrow. And Reb Zalman, who had also seen those faces in the flames, embraced Hayim Elya and reassured him. And when Hayim Elya became calm, he turned to Reb Zalman and said: "But Rebbe, how is it possible that I have seen these faces, so beloved and so much missed?" And then, for the first time, Reb Zalman explained the mystery of that menorah, and he said: "The menorah downstairs represents this world, while the menorah that burns on the second floor represents the world on high. Therefore when we peer into the flames of these candles we are able to invoke spirits from the world to come.

"Now spirits surround us all the time, especially those spirits of the departed whom we love, but they are invisible to us, because spirits do not have a visible body. However, the flame of the candle is one medium in which it is possible for the faces of the spirits to reveal themselves, as has just happened to you. And they are able to make themselves known to us through this menorah in particular, for to sit before these flames is to invoke the forces that exist on high."

Hayim Elya was truly amazed at this explanation, which might have seemed impossible to him an hour before, but which now seemed completely reasonable. And after that Reb Zalman revealed the reason that he took his place in front of the candles of that menorah to the other Hasidim, and the next year, when *Hanukah* returned, they too peered into those flames, and saw the faces of those spirits that surrounded them. And after that this practice became a *minhag* of all of the Hasidim of Reb Zalman, and it is still observed to this day.

THE MITZVAH AUCTION

for Moshe Waldocks

I n every generation there are thirty-six hidden *Tzaddikim.* They are the pillars on which the world stands, for it is the existence of these hidden saints that causes God to temper his justice with mercy. And without God's mercy, the world would soon fall sway to the *Yetzer Hara,* the Evil Inclination, and before long it would be as with the generation of Noah, who were destroyed.

Now the truth is that while the identity of these thirty-six *Tzaddikim,* known as the *Lamed-vav,* is hidden from the world at large, it is not completely secret. For the rebbes of the world—those *Tzaddikim* who are not required to stay hidden—are able to seek out these righteous ones, since their pure souls communicate with each other in dreams. And then it is the duty of the rebbe to see to it that the needs of that *Tzaddik* and his family are met. For when their lives flourish, so does the world, but when they suffer, the world suffers as well.

Now in Zholkiev there were three such hidden saints. The sacred duty of attending to them had belonged to Reb Avraham Yehoshua, of blessed memory. After his death Reb

Zalman himself cared for them for many years. But he always gave the task of raising funds for these hidden ones to one of his Hasidim, who vied among themselves for this honor. What the Hasidim loved, in particular, was running the *Mitzvah* auction that raised funds for the hidden *Tzaddikim*. Here *aliyahs* for the whole year were parceled out, and the Hasidim believed that such a contract, made months in advance, assured that they would live at least until it was fulfilled. Therefore the *aliyahs* coming in the latter months were the first to be sold, and those of the nearest period, the last.

That year Reb Zalman gave the task and honor to Reb Moshe Shor-Habar who, like Reb Naftali of Ropshitz, could remove the scowl from the face and the lock from the heart. The auction took place in its usual jovial way, for everyone was delighted to purchase such precious *mitzvot*. Yet, when all the *aliyahs* for the next twelve months had been sold, and every instance of taking the Torah out of the Ark, or carrying the Torah around the synagogue on *Sukkos* was gone, Reb Moshe still had not raised enough to sustain the hidden *Tzaddikim* for one year. Therefore he decided to enlarge the auction. First he called Reb Shlomo, the *hazan*, over to him and asked if he would be willing to sell two unwritten *nigunim* to the highest bidder, for the sake of the hidden ones. Of course Reb Shlomo agreed—for with the aid of the pure souls of the hidden ones, he would no doubt bring back a *nigun* from *Gan Eden*.

Then Reb Moshe offered up Reb Shlomo's *nigunim*, and they sold at a very high price. After that Reb Moshe asked Reb Hayim Elya if he would copy out the unprinted portion of Hayim Vital's *Sha'ar Hakedusha* for the highest bidder. And again the bidding for the manuscript was very high, for it dealt with the acquisition of vision. Then, with a twinkle in his eye, Reb Moshe asked Reb Zalman if he would promise to offer a special prayer for whoever purchased that *mitzvah*, and Reb Zalman nodded his approval. And of course this blessing was the most sought after, for everyone knew how powerful were Reb Zalman's prayers.

After this every Hasid was approached by Reb Moshe to contribute one such *mitzvah*, with which to aid another. And all joyfully gave these, for the *mitzvah* of performing any one of them was in itself a great blessing. And in each case Reb Moshe managed to request something that the Hasid would love to be able to give.

Reb Hanan offered the *mitzvah* of reminding everyone that we have a Father in heaven who loves us. This *mitzvah* was purchased by Reb David. Reb Yosef offered to copy out eighteen teachings on the *Amidah* that he had collected from various rebbes. That sold for eighteen silver pieces. Reb Benzion Moshe offered to serve as the order keeper and announcer at two weddings, and this honor was snatched up by a father who still had two unwed daughters. As for Reb Moshe himself, he was also a fine violinist, and he offered to play *nigunim* on the violin for a *bris.* And three Hasidim who were expectant fathers tried to outbid each other for this *mitzvah,* for in buying it they hoped to assure that they *would* have a *bris.*

So it went for hours and hours that day in Zholkiev, with Reb Moshe regaling them with stories, puns and jokes, and needless to say Reb Moshe was always selected, from then on, to run the *Mitzvah* auction. So too was it certain that for as long as he did the lives of the hidden *Tzaddikim* flourished, and so did the lives of the people.

A MIDWIFE FOR SOULS

for Shalvi and Khaya

There was a young girl whose name was Shulamit who lived in a mountain village in Southern Germany where very few Jews were to be found. And although this girl was only twelve years old, the longing of her spirit for God was very great, and as long as she could remember she had been praying to God for a sign.

In those days Reb Zalman passed through the village while on a long journey to visit the grave of the Baal Shem of Michelstadt, and joined the *Minyan* in that town for *Minhah* on Friday afternoon, even though he did not know where he would be spending the *Shabbas*. Now the *Minyan* in that village was very loyal, for there was barely a *Minyan* of Jewish men living there, and if one of them were to stay home, there would not be enough left for a *Minyan*. But it happened that one of those men was sick that day, and that Reb Zalman had the honor of being the tenth man. And from that moment on Reb Zalman knew that he need fear for nothing, for whenever one has the honor of the tenth man it is a sign that God is watching over him.

So it was that after *Minhah* and *Maariv* Reb Zalman was invited by one of the men in the *Minyan* to stay at his home for the Sabbath. And that man was the father of the girl Shulamit. And one of the reasons that he invited him was that there were no Hasidim to be found in the village, and he wanted his daughter to know something of the Hasidim, for he himself was a great admirer of the tales and teachings of the Baal Shem Tov.

Now all during the *Shabbas* dinner Shulamit was very silent, and rarely looked up from her plate. But Reb Zalman was aware from the first that there was something unusual about her, for she was far more intense than other children her age. And after the meal Reb Zalman turned to her and said: "Is there something you would like to ask me?" Then the young girl found the confidence to speak, and she said: "Would you please tell me a story? I've been waiting for someone to tell me a story. I need to hear a story." And this is the story that Reb Zalman told her:

"Once upon a time there was a young girl who was young on the outside but old on the inside. Now this girl had a special destiny, for she had been given a particular task by God to do, but no one who knew her believed it was more than a fantasy. Therefore this young girl waited for a sign from God to confirm her calling. Yet, though she expected that sign to come at any time, nothing out of the ordinary seemed to happen. Still, she never gave up hope for her special calling.

"And what calling was this? This young girl believed that it was her destiny to become a midwife. But not only a midwife to women, but a midwife to every one in the world. For there are some babies that are born from the belly, and others that are born from the heart. And when she would say to her parents that she wanted to be a midwife to babies that are born from the heart, they would laugh and think her merely naive. They did not understand at all that she knew what she was saying, for she had been born with a wonderful intuition that let her perceive her destiny long before it manifested itself.

"And so it was that in the end she did indeed become such a midwife for souls, for she helped all those whom she encountered in bringing forth the child in their heart that was waiting to be born."

Here Reb Zalman ended the story, and he saw that tears were flowing from the girl's eyes, and everyone wondered why she was crying. And Reb Zalman alone among them knew the reason for her tears, for the story he had told her was her own story, and it was also the sign that she had been awaiting so long.

All the next day, during *Shabbas,* Shulamit smiled and glowed as if the Sabbath Queen were her closest friend. Her parents had never seen her so happy and at peace with herself, and they thought that she must be happy to have a visitor stay with them since so few visitors passed their way.

And that night, as Shulamit held the *Havdolah* candle and Reb Zalman stood beside her, she whispered to him: "How did you know?" And Reb Zalman replied: "If you listen hard enough it is possible to hear the angels as they whisper among themselves. Now on the Sabbath everyone is accompanied by two angels, and during the dinner I heard one angel tell another about your future destiny. And when you asked me to tell a tale, I thought that you might have been dimly aware of overhearing the angels, and what you were really asking is that I repeat what they had said. So I did." And when Shulamit heard this, the glow that surrounded her face became as bright as the flame of the candle, for then she knew for certain that it was indeed her destiny to serve as a midwife for souls. And that is exactly what she grew up to be.

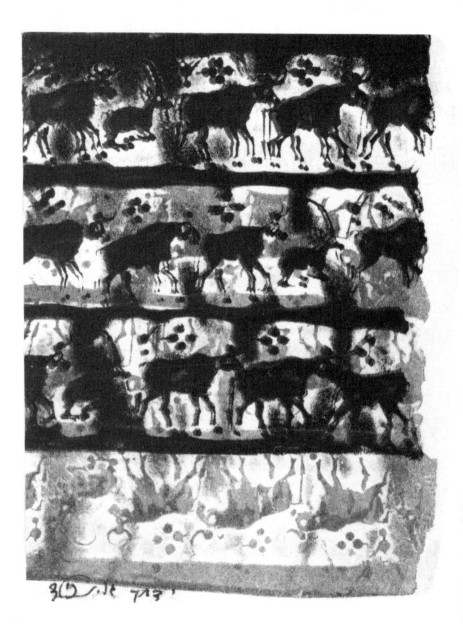

THE SUNRISE SERVICE

for Rabbi Shlomo Carlebach

O nce a group of ten Hasidim were sent by their Rebbe, Reb Shlomo, to seek out Reb Zalman and to ask him to teach them about *davening,* for Reb Zalman was widely recognized as a *Baal Tefillah,* a master of prayer. Reb Zalman agreed to teach them, but made them promise in advance to do whatever he asked of them, no manner how strange it might seem, and the Hasidim agreed to these conditions. Then Reb Zalman asked to know when they prayed on *Shabbas* morning, and the Hasidim told him that they liked to be well rested, so they met at ten o'clock in the morning. Then Reb Zalman said: "What is the first thing that you say when you start to *daven?*" And they replied: "Blessed art Thou, O Lord our God, King of the Universe, who gives the rooster discrimination to know the difference between day and night." Then Reb Zalman said: "Why don't you meet the rooster when the rooster awakes?"

Therefore Reb Zalman awoke the Hasidim before sunrise, and as soon as they had dressed he told them to follow him. But he did not lead them to the *Beit Knesset,* as they expected, but into the nearby forest, where they walked until they reached a clearing on a hill, facing East. The Hasidim were quite surprised by this, for they had never prayed outdoors. After all, where was the Ark for them to face, with the scroll of the Torah inside it? But they had given Reb Zalman their word that they would obey without questioning, so they kept their misgivings to themselves.

So it was that the Hasidim turned to the East and prayed *Shaharis* that day in that place, surrounded by the birds and animals that awoke in the forest around them. And it had been so long since they had stood in one place in a forest that they were restored to nature, and thus their prayers were said with a clarity and depth that had often been missing. And it was due to that very absence that Reb Shlomo had sent them to see Reb Zalman.

Thus when Reb Zalman brought them back to that forest clearing the next morning, they did not hesitate to go, for they had so benefited from praying in that place. Now in the past each one of them had focused on his own prayers above all, but that day, for some reason, they found themselves aware of how all of their prayers were linked together, and rose up as one. And it was almost as if they were able to see the crown woven on high from their intermingled prayers. And that day they felt a part of the community of Israel as they had never felt before, and knew that the effect of all of their prayers rising upward was very great. And they came to realize how all of those prayers formed the limbs of the Divine Presence in this world.

The third morning, as well, Reb Zalman led the *Minyan* back into the forest. This time he had them *daven* in groups of two. And before they began, he said: "There is a spark of the Divine in every person. So when you *daven* together, address the Divine in your partner, and let your partner address the Divine in you. And for today you must each alternate in pronouncing the lines of the prayers: one will say one line and the other the next. And when the other is speaking, listen as closely as if you had pronounced the words yourself." This the Hasidim did, and their prayers that day were shared between two in a way they had never known. So too did they hear the prayers themselves in a new manner, for now they heard each line individually as well as part of the whole. And they gained a deeper understanding of the mysteries of the prayers, which they had never previously known.

On the fourth morning Reb Zalman led the Hasidim back to the clearing for the last time. There he said: "Know that I have been trying to guide you through the gates of *Pardes*. The first of these gates is *Peshat,* that of the literal. And on the first morning here you came to know the *Peshat* of prayer, which once rose up as spontaneously as the song of the bird or the crowing of the rooster. On the second morning we entered the second gate of *Pardes,* that of *Remez,* which permits a glimpse into a still more profound meaning. And that day you glimpsed how the prayers of Israel form the limbs of the Divine Presence.

"Yesterday we considered *davening* from the perspective of the gate of *Drash,* in which more than one meaning is found, and you began to perceive how prayers can be understood in many different ways. Today, our last day together, I would like to lead you through the gate of *Sod,* that of Mystery."

Then, just as Reb Zalman finished speaking, the sun appeared on the horizon, and the Hasidim began to pray. And that day their prayers blended together the songs of the birds around them with those of their rebbe, Reb Shlomo, into a wonderful symphony. And as they prayed, each one came to recognize that his own contribution was like that of one of the instruments of the symphony, and that the prayers they sang out were its notes. And before they finished *davening* that morning, they heard as well the voices of the angels who joined them in those prayers, which they had never heard in all the days of their lives. And thus they came to recognize how all life, in the worlds above and below, serves as a great chorus giving praise to the Holy One for all the blessings He has bestowed.

REB ZALMAN AND
REB MALACH HAMOVES

for Herb Walker

M any were those who brought their yearnings, as well as their despair, to Reb Zalman. He often gave a blessing, as when he blessed the unborn child of Reb Hayim Elya by placing his hands on the belly of Tselya, Hayim Elya's wife, and pronouncing the blessings. And that child, Nussan, was a healthy and happy one. So too did Reb Zalman often travel by wagon from one town to another, where on the day before the Sabbath he would meet with those in pain. Then he would prepare for the Sabbath, and offer a *D'var Torah* on *Shabbas*. And before the Sabbath ended he would entrust the sufferings that he had heard to the dove of the *Shekhinah*, to carry heavenward for him. And inevitably those prayers were heard on high.

Then one day, as Reb Zalman started to walk out of his house, about to leave for another *Shtetl*, he stood next to the *Mezzuzah* and hesitated for a moment. Then he turned to Reb Simcha and said: "Please take my bags back into my room. I'm not going to go there." Then he said to Reb Sholem: "Please go to Reb Shmuel Leib and ask him to go to that town in my place. For as I stood before the *Mezzuzah*, I saw the *Malach*

Hamoves. And I said to him: "Why do you stand here and threaten me?" And the Angel of Death replied: 'Is it not written in the Torah that he who desecrates the Sabbath will surely die?' And I said 'Wherever I go I teach about keeping the *Shabbas.*' And the *Malach Hamoves* said: 'Yes, but when do you rest?' It was then that I knew that I couldn't go."

So Reb Shmuel Leib went on Reb Zalman's behalf and Reb Zalman stayed home, and he remained in his room alone. For his Hasidim had not expected him to be there for *Shabbas,* and in any case it was required that he rest. That afternoon Reb Zalman went to the *Mikvah,* and when he returned to his room he lay down to rest a bit before *Shabbas* began. But almost at once he fell into a deep sleep, and he slept through all of Friday night, for no one wanted to wake him, and he did not wake up until *Shabbas* morning. The first thing he heard was the sound of *davening* from downstairs, and he knew that they had begun without him. Then he went and took his father's *tallis* and wrapped himself in it and turned to the Holy One, blessed be He, and said: "I was not able to meet the Sabbath bride, nor did I join the others in *davening.* What is it that I can offer You?" Then, as he stood there with his hands raised up before him, Reb Zalman saw that his hands seemed to form the word *Kadosh,* holiness, and in that instant a vision opened to him, and he saw the holiness inherent in the simple things of the world: the sparks of holiness reflecting from the grain growing in the fields and of the apples growing on trees, the holiness of the river that he saw from his window, and the holiness of the rain and the wind. And as he stood there, he placed his hands on his heart, and he heard the sound *Kadosh, Kadosh* pulsing through all of creation. And when he raised his hands to his head and let them cover his eyes, he saw a vision of the holiness of all kinds of relationships: the holiness of father and child, of child and mother, of mother and father, of grandfather and grandchild, of friend and friend, of lover and lover, of the covenant between those who wed according to the law of Moses and of Israel, and of the promises made to those who are dying, and of every kind of covenant.

This led him to see a vision of the holy light of the robe of the *Shekhinah* in which the world is wrapped. And there he saw illumined every idea of truth and freedom and of goodness and blessing, and he saw the world with a clarity such as he had never known. The holiness of the holy overwhelmed him and he raised his hands to a still higher place and he heard the *Kadosh* sung by the seraphim. And when he stood for the *Amidah* he felt the fullness of God's glory in all worlds. And yet he knew that all that glory, which was immeasurable, was nothing more than the rays of the sun in comparison to the sun itself, before whom they were insignificant. And there he saw the letters of the Torah written across the heavens as Moses must have seen them at Sinai. And after that he fell back to sleep, and slept through the rest of *Shabbas* and only woke just before sunset.

And as he woke Reb Zalman heard a voice whispering, and the voice said that in all the hurry to bring the *Mashiach* and to care for others and to give out blessings, it was also necessary not to forget to find the island of peace that is the essence of *Shabbas*. And while he listened to those words, recognizing their truth, at first he did not know who had said them. But suddenly he recognized the voice. And after that it became a *minhag* that Reb Zalman kept every fourth *Shabbas* alone. And when others asked where he had learned that such a tradition was necessary, he would reply, "That is the Torah I learned from Reb *Malach Hamoves.*"

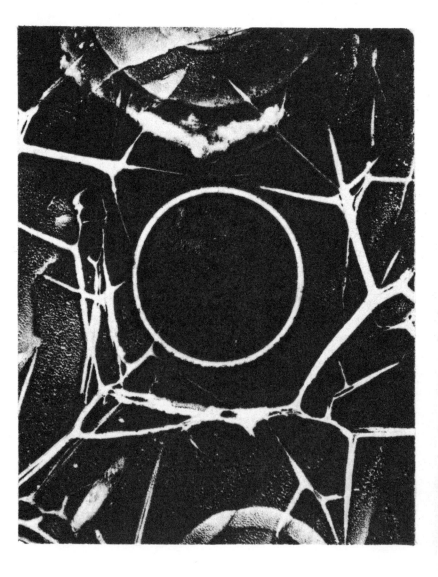

THE COUNCIL OF THE ELDERS

for Matya Yonah

After his encounter with Reb *Malach Hamoves*, the Angel of Death, Reb Zalman knew that the shadow of death still hung over him, and he resolved to fulfill the commandment *Thou shalt rest.* That night Reb Zalman dreamed that forty Sabbaths came to him and said: "Take leave of your friends and your family and follow us, and we promise to give you every rest stop of the desert, as it is written, *they traveled and they rested.*" And Reb Zalman had packed his *tallis* and *tefillin* and had begun to follow them, when he awoke. After that he told his family and his Hasidim that he had decided to go off alone into the forest for forty days and nights, and that including the day of his departure and the day of his return he would be gone for forty-two days.

Now it happened that as Reb Zalman took leave of his son and daughter-in-law, who was with child, his son said: "What will we do if a grandchild is born to you during this period? For surely you must be present in the event of a *bris.*" But Reb Zalman told them that it would not be fitting for him to welcome a grandchild with the shadow of death still hanging over him, and he assured them that God would bring them together at the right moment.

Then Reb Zalman took his *tallis* and *tefillin* and a small notebook in which to write words of the Torah that might come down to him, and set out alone. His family begged him to take some provisions, but he assured them that God would provide. And as he departed, Reb Zalman saw a strange sight near the entrance of his home: There were a great cluster of caterpillars, whose color was radiant green. And Reb Zalman knew that this must be a sign. Therefore he stopped and counted the caterpillars, and there were forty in all. And he knew that this meant he had been given forty days for his retreat.

Just then the forty caterpillars began to move, scurrying off at remarkable pace, and when he saw this Reb Zalman decided that he would follow them, for he was very curious to know where they were going. He found that he had to walk briskly, but not run, in order to keep up with the caterpillars, who wriggled their way through the thicket and headed for the forest. After an hour Reb Zalman came to a wooden hut far in the woods, which he had never known about, with an esrog tree planted in front of it. It was there that the caterpillars stopped, and Reb Zalman knew that this would be his home.

Indeed, the hut was empty except for a chair, a table, a bed and an oil lamp. Everything was worn but well preserved. And on closer inspection Reb Zalman also found a number of dry herbs. Outside the hut he examined the fruit that grew from that esrog tree, for he was amazed to find it growing there, and he knew that it must have been planted by a Jew.

Reb Zalman tasted the fruit of the esrog, and instead of that which is usually found, being very bitter and pulpy, that esrog was extremely juicy and delicious. And Reb Zalman knew that he was blessed indeed to have come there. Just then, however, the wind began to blow through the trees, and to his complete amazement Reb Zalman found that he could understand the words of the wind, which told him that the

Baal Shem Tov had once lived there. And then Reb Zalman understood that the fruit of that esrog had been planted with the blessings of the Baal Shem Tov, and that is why it was so delicious. And it must have also happened that tasting the fruit let him taste of the Baal Shem's blessings, and that is why he had been able to understand the wind.

Just then Reb Zalman heard a terrible howling, which greatly frightened him, for he had not expected to encounter evil in that place. He turned on his heels and ran into the hut as fast as he could, and closed the door and locked it. And from the window he looked outside, to see where the howling had come from. And to his complete amazement he saw that the house was surrounded by demons, forty in all, who were howling in the wind every extraneous thought that had ever interrupted him while praying, every desire that did not seem right to fulfill, and every urge that had from time to time invaded him. And among those demons was Lilith, who caught his eye and began to undress before him, hoping to entice him to come out of the hut. One moment she was dressed in the most desirable finery, and the next moment her raiment was gone, and she stood naked before him. But Reb Zalman turned his eyes away and recited one of the psalms, and when he raised his eyes again she was gone, replaced by another demon. And Reb Zalman recognized that demon—it was one of his own. And as the howling demons arrayed themselves closer to the hut, Reb Zalman recognized each and every one. For those were not someone else's demons, or demons that came from somewhere else to plague him, but demons that he himself had nurtured through his neglect in weeding his own garden. And Reb Zalman suddenly realized that they surrounded him all the time, but that by eating that esrog he was now able to see them. And he knew as well that even as those demons were like weeds, so even weeds had some medicinal value. And he prayed that he might gain the knowledge and understanding of how they had come to haunt him, and how he might deliver himself from their curse.

Then Reb Zalman saw that the forty caterpillars were forming a circle around the house, and the demons rushed to get out of that circle as fast as they could. And Reb Zalman knew that the caterpillars had formed a circle that could not be broken, an *Eruv*, or boundary, in which he would be protected. Then Reb Zalman regained his confidence and cautiously went outside. And outside that circle, at its edge, he saw the demons clustered together, howling for his attention, but unable to come any closer.

Then Reb Zalman returned to the hut, and since night was falling he sought to light the lamp. Now there was no oil to be found in the house, except for a small amount in the lamp itself Reb Zalman did not expect it to last for very long, but he felt that he needed light to expel the presence of those demons. In any case, Reb Zalman had nothing with which to light the lamp. He did not know what he could do, for he could not go beyond the protected circle as long as the demons were there. He looked around the hut some more, and opened the stove. To his amazement, he found one glowing ember inside it, impossible as that seemed. And he took a straw and lit it, and with the straw he lit the lamp. And the light cast by that lamp filled the room with warmth as well. And all the time Reb Zalman was there he felt as if the light of the *Shekhinah* shone upon him. And that lamp did not burn out during all the forty days that followed, neither did the ember stop glowing.

With the house illumined, the howling of the demons could no longer be heard. Then Reb Zalman realized that the esrog fruit was the only thing he had eaten that day. Just then he noticed a basket in one corner of that room, and when he picked it up he found that it was filled with carobs. Reb Zalman was delighted to find them, for carobs had been the food eaten by Rabbi Shimon bar Yohai and his son, Rabbi Eliezer, during the thirteen years they had spent in a cave, hiding from the Romans and writing the Zohar. If carobs had sustained Rabbi Shimon for thirteen years, they would surely sustain Reb Zalman for forty days.

Then Reb Zalman counted the carobs, and lo and behold there were forty in all, and he resolved to eat one a day, and nothing more, except for the fruit of that delicious esrog tree. And he knew that in this way he would surely purify his body in that time. Now Reb Zalman found that carob not only as delicious as manna, but also remarkably filling, as if he had eaten a full meal. Then he realized that he was tired, for he had come a long way, and had been confronted with his own howling demons. And he felt like sleeping. So he went over to the bed and lay down on it, and as soon as he closed his eyes, he slept.

Now that night Reb Zalman had an astonishing dream in which he found himself in a desert filled with rubble. Reb Zalman wondered where he was, and what it was that he was walking on, that shattered with every step he took. He picked up a piece of it, and found that it looked like a shard of a broken vessel. Then, in the dream, he noticed a stream flowing nearby, but rather than flowing with water, it gave off a wonderful scent, as if some kind of nectar flowed there. And when Reb Zalman saw that flowing stream, with its wonderful odor, he realized that he was very thirsty, and he wanted to drink.

Then Reb Zalman bent over the stream, and cupped his hands and tried to fill them, but the liquid ran out of his hands. Reb Zalman tried again and again, but he could not hold on to even a drop of it. Just then he looked down and saw that there was something written on one of the shards near his hands. He picked it up and found that the words were written in Hebrew, and it said: "Whoever would taste this nectar must first find an unbroken vessel and fill it."

Reb Zalman considered these words, and realized that the shards he had been walking on must all be broken vessels, and that he must somehow restore one of them if he wanted to drink that water. But how on earth could such a shattered vessel be restored? Just then Reb Zalman awoke, with the dream still vivid to him, and its meaning manifested itself to him as if the spirit of Joseph were with him. And he understood that in order to restore himself he must find a way to restore one of the shattered vessels of which the Ari spoke.

Then Reb Zalman remembered hearing that demons were actually imperfect angels. And it occurred to him that in this case the demons were not unlike the broken vessels, for both required *tikkun* in order to be restored. And all at once Reb Zalman vowed, with great *kavanah*, to do everything in his power to repair those demons, and turn them back into angels.

So Reb Zalman set about to try to think of a way in which the demons might be metamorphosed into angels. For even imperfect angels would be much better than those howling demons. In the meantime he realized that he was very thirsty, but where was he to find anything to drink? Reb Zalman looked around the hut once more, and this time he saw a jug in one corner, which he had not noticed before. He went over, picked it up, and pulled out the stopper, and a wonderful odor rose up to him, one that he recalled at once—it was the very same odor as the nectar in his dream! Reb Zalman could hardly believe his luck. He hurriedly got a cup and poured out some of the nectar, said the blessing, and then tasted it, offering a *L'hayim* to the demons clustered outside the charmed circle. And the taste of that nectar was so delectable that Reb Zalman never forgot it for the rest of his life, and when he mentioned it he always called it the *schnaps* of Eden, and he was certain that it must have been the favorite drink of the angels. And that, indeed, is what it was.

Reb Zalman felt himself considerably calmed and warmed by that first sip, and his thirst no longer plagued him. He arose and went to the window and looked out. He still did not consider going outside, for he wanted to remain within that protected circle. (In fact, nothing could have tempted him to step outside it at that point.) Reb Zalman recalled the tales about Reb Adam and the Baal Shem Tov, both of whom protected themselves inside a magical circle, such as those said to have been drawn by Solomon. And he knew full well that he was inside such a charmed circle—which Reb Zalman now saw consisted of forty cocoons—where he need fear nothing. And he fully intended to remain there.

Now the cries of the demons could still be heard, but they seemed slightly less hysterical, as if they too had been calmed in some way. Reb Zalman considered this, and decided to take another sip of that heavenly *schnaps*, while keeping his eyes on the demons outside. And by doing this a few times, Reb Zalman was able to determine that there was an exact correlation between his taking those sips and the calming process that finally caused the demons to quiet down, and for a dim light to appear around their faces for the first time. And when Reb Zalman saw this light, he was thrilled, for he recognized it as the light they had lost when, due to his neglect, they had fallen, as angels, from the celestial heights. And he realized that somehow he had caused the falling to stop, and that now it was a matter of making it possible for them to learn how to ascend once more, something they no longer knew how to do by themselves.

Now that was the eve of the first Sabbath of his solitude, and Reb Zalman was filled with longing to greet the Sabbath Queen. And for a while he forgot about transforming the demons into angels, and turned his thoughts to the higher realm. And that night he sang all the Sabbath songs and said all the prayers out loud, even though he was alone. And yet he did not feel alone, as he had feared, but rather that he was, in fact, sharing that *Shabbas*. Reb Zalman could not help noting his absence of loneliness, and then he realized that he felt as if he were sharing that Sabbath with those imperfect angels.

And the next morning, indeed, when Reb Zalman looked out the window at the first light, he saw that the demons had sprouted wings—sagging, pathetic wings, it is true, but wings nevertheless. And he knew that the power of the Sabbath had somehow reached them, and was making it possible for them to be returned to the form they had before they had fallen. And then it occurred to him that this process was indeed like that of restoring a jug from all those scattered shards. And he suddenly realized that the jug he had drunk from must be one that his soul had repaired, for he was quite positive it had not been there when he looked around the hut at first. And because he had succeeded in repairing that one vessel, it was now possible for the broken vessels of those fallen angels to be restored as well.

So it was that Reb Zalman devoted himself fully to the task of healing those forty imperfect angels—for, in fact, they no longer could be called demons. At first he intended to pray for the benefit of all of them at the same time. But then it came to him in a flash of inspiration that he should devote one day to each one, since they were the same number. This he did, and each day he turned all his love and devotion for the Torah towards healing one of those fallen angels, reciting psalms for it without end. And lo and behold by the end of the first day the angel's countenance was beaming, its wings perfect, and it was able to take flight towards the heavens. And Reb Zalman knew that for every one of them that was restored to the heights, his soul received an immeasurable blessing, for the Lord delights in the recovery of a fallen angel as much as He does in that of a fallen human being.

In this way the forty days he lived in that hut were spent in concentration and devotion. And at the end of each day Reb Zalman had the great blessing of seeing one of those angels taking flight, bearing Reb Zalman's own prayers heavenward. And when the time came, on the last day, for him to release the last angel, he did, and it soared heavenward. And just then the cocoons of the caterpillars cracked open, and a golden butterfly emerged out of each one. These butterflies assembled at once into a flock and set off flying, and when Reb Zalman saw this, he hurried outside of the charmed circle for the first time since he had come there, and followed that flock of butterflies wherever it went. For those caterpillars had not led him astray and neither, he was certain, would those butterflies.

The butterflies led Reb Zalman a great distance, so that sometimes he had to rest along the way. In fact, he found that he made forty-two rest stops, exactly as had the Children of Israel in their desert wanderings. They traveled all night, and by the morning Reb Zalman reached the mountain at the far side of that huge forest. And the trees that grew there were very old, even ancient, and as the wind blew through them they seemed to speak, and he thought he heard them say: "Welcome, Reb Zalman, on this, your sixtieth birthday, into the Council of the Elders." And when Reb Zalman heard this, he suddenly remembered that it was indeed his birthday that day, and that he had completed fifty-nine years, although he had forgotten about it completely in his concern to transform the demons into angels. So too did he wonder what was the Council of the Elders of which they spoke. And just then, in the shadow of one mountain, Reb Zalman saw a majestic figure, into whose presence he had been led. And now Reb Zalman ran forward to meet his fate; no longer did he hide his face from it.

And there, in the shadow of the mountain, the voice of a great prophet addressed him—for it was none other than Moses the Redeemer himself. And Reb Zalman understood at once that this was how Moses had addressed all of those assembled at Sinai at the same time, for his words echoed from the mountain and filled the forest. And Moses said to him: "Welcome, Zalman, on this, the first day of your sixtieth year. Know that the pain and experience of the past has turned to wisdom; and the great love that you hold shall be turned into blessings that you can give, for now you have joined the Council of the Elders." Then Moses said, with the loving inflections of a father: "Zalman, Zalman, you are not even half of my age, but know that I was sixty years old at the time that I met Zipporah my wife. Know too that from this day on you will have added to your name the word *Zaida*, and thus you have become *Zaida* Zalman." And when he heard this, Reb Zalman knew that he must have become a grandfather, and a great joy filled his heart.

Then Moses said: "Take hold of my hand." This Reb Zalman did, and with his other hand Moses pointed up to the sky, where Reb Zalman saw the Ten Commandments inscribed in black fire on white. And Moses pointed to the commandment *Thou shalt honor thy father and mother*, and he

said: "Look closely at this commandment." And when Reb
Zalman did this, he saw written beneath it the words "Honor
thy grandfather and grandmother as well." And Moses said:
"Those words were written there all along, but you had not
reached the age where you could see them. Now they stand
revealed to you."

Then Moses said: "Know, Zalman, that the world stands
in great need of blessings. Therefore you have been ap-
pointed to the Council of Elders to see that these blessings are
given, and not only to the young, but to the old as well. And
fear not that you have become too old to bear the Tabernacle
on your shoulders—the time has come for you to serve as a
source of blessings and knowledge, and not to carry burdens." And Reb Zalman was filled with the greatest peace on
hearing these words, and he replied, with all his heart,
"Amen."

Then Reb Zalman saw that Moses was about to take his
leave. And he was overcome with longing to speak with
Moses about questions of the Law that had long haunted him.
And Moses, who read these thoughts in his face, replied: "You
may ask me one question, and I will willingly reply, unless it
concerns the time of the coming of the Messiah, which I am
not permitted to reveal."

Then Reb Zalman asked the question that was closest to
his heart. For he did believe with perfect faith in the coming
of the Messiah, as stated in the twelfth principle of
Maimonides. And he said: "I have long wondered on many
questions, but this one above all: When the Messiah comes it
is known that the Temple will be rebuilt for the third and final
time. But how will this take place without destroying the
mosque that has been built on that holiest site?" And Moses
smiled a great smile, which Reb Zalman never forgot for as
long as a single second for the rest of his life.

And Moses said: "Even now the Temple is being restored
far under the earth by the prayers and longings of Israel. Your
own prayers, Reb Zalman, during the past forty days, have
gone very far in restoring the Holy of Holies itself, the place
of the Ark of the Covenant. And when the Temple has been

completely restored this way, then the time of the Messiah will have arrived, and the Temple will rise up out of the earth, in all its glory, for the whole world to see. And as it rises up there will be a wing of the Temple for each nation of the world, and that is why it is written *My house shall be called the House of Prayer for all nations.*"

Then Moses took his leave and turned and walked into the shadow of the mountain and disappeared from Reb Zalman's eyes. And all at once he heard the fluttering of the butterflies, and saw that they were departing. Then he did not hesitate, but followed them, and they led him directly back to his home in Zholkiev. And no sooner did Reb Zalman arrive home, than his son came out of the door and embraced him and there were tears of joy in his eyes. For he had been blessed with a son, and Reb Zalman had returned on that, his forty-second day, which was also the eighth day since the birth, and the day of the *bris*.

So it was that Reb Zalman had the honor of serving as the *mohel* at the Covenant of his own grandson. And when he did, he knew that he had not only received a great blessing from Moses, Our Redeemer, but that he had also been permitted to transmit that great blessing to this, his first grandchild. And he saw then how correct Moses had been about the blessings of old age, which he had never before known.

APPENDIX A

Reb Yonassan, who visited many tribes and peoples, and knew many languages, was present at the deathbed of Hannah Rochel, the "Maid of Ludmir." It was from her that he learned of the meeting that had taken place between Reb Zalman and herself. When Reb Yonassan returned to Zholkiev, he told Reb Zalman all that he had heard from her, and Reb Zalman, deeply moved, told Reb Yonassan the rest of the story. All that he heard from each of them was recorded by Reb Yonassan in a long letter that he sent to Reb Hayim Elya. This letter is here printed in full, so that the events of this remarkable meeting shall be preserved.

THE TORAH

OF THE MENORAH

Wh
hen Reb Zalman of Zholkiev had first heard of
Hannah Rochel, the "Maid of Ludmir," he
wondered why the blessed *Shekhinah* did not have more such
holy representatives. It seemed to him right that there should
be female rebbes as well as male ones—after all, were not
many of the judges and prophets of old also women?

But when he later heard how the other rebbes in
her neighborhood of the Tzar's country had strongly dis-
approved, and heaped indignities upon her, Reb Zalman was
gravely troubled. In his deeper meditations he had learned
that she was indeed a great Zaddik, a very holy soul who had
undertaken to prepare the way for other female Zaddikim yet
to come. Because all beginnings are difficult, she had know-
ingly taken this task as her own—fully aware that she would
meet with opposition. For her courage, Reb Zalman respected
her greatly, but he also knew that his own mission would be
jeopardized if he openly stood at her side.

Oy, there was now so much bickering, so much fighting
among the Hassidim. Disputes between the Zanzer and the

Sadigorer, between the followers of the Strelisker and the Premishlaner...where now was the joyous path of the Baal Shem Tov? Some persons, devoid of the holy light, had chosen to be particularly strict in observing the *mitzvot* of judgment, and now, alas, these over-zealous rebbes had decreed on the Maid of Ludmir to marry. As if that restriction could quench her burning light! But after a brief, unconsummated marriage, she was divorced, and the painful suffering of all this made her decide to leave Europe and travel to the Holy Land. There, in solitude, she would be able to devote herself fully to the service of the *Shekhinah*.

Reb Zalman was now filled with a longing to meet her face-to-face. He summoned Feivel the Dark and Feivel the Light to accompany him, without first telling them of his intention. Only after they had gone some miles from Zholkiev did Reb Zalman reveal his quest. Now they understood why their rebbe had not dressed like a rabbi, and he pledged them to conceal his identity. He would pose as a merchant, traveling with two apprentices to buy goods in a distant city.

Reb Zalman trusted that God lead them to the encounter, for he knew not where to go, since Hannah Rochel, too, had veiled herself and was traveling in disguise. He knew only that she was going through the Kaiser's country to the Holy Land, accompanied by a devoted widow who served as her personal attendant. Beyond that, he could only follow the road wherever it might lead.

It was mid-November, that change-of-seasons time between the gathering of the harvest and the arrival of winter. The air was cold and crisp, with frosty winds that long ago had blown the leaves to the forest floor. Reb Zalman and his companions watched the last flights of birds wing their way southward over the stark bare branches of the sleeping trees. The sharp contrast of the dark tree trunks against the sky reminded them of ink on paper, like a kind of primal script written by the hand of God in a language long forgotten, a script that moved and danced, swirling and blurring into the white-on-white nothingness of pre-creation.

It was no vision, but a sudden blizzard, come upon them while they were dozing. Now the snow had covered the road, growing deeper and deeper, making travel impossible. Reb Zalman wanted to leave the wagon and proceed on foot, but Feivel the Light, wise in the ways of the Northland, counseled against it. One could freeze to death in a matter of hours. Better to pull off into that grove of evergreens, unhitch the horse so he could turn his back to the wind, and wait out the storm together. Good idea...but as they turned, it seemed as if the wagon had begun to spin, as if they were carried by the storm into the timeless void...How long? Who knows? But when the storm ended, they did not recognize the little town in the valley below.

Baruch Hashem—there was an inn, with warmth and food and a stable for the horse. Inside they met two women, also lost in the storm, and yes, it was Hannah Rochel and her companion. Reb Zalman was overjoyed, and, as it would not become them to have a private conversation behind closed doors, they sat at one table in the corner of the room, in full view but out of earshot of the others.

They spoke of the souls of women and their service to God, about the timebound commandments from which women are exempt, about the prayers in *tehinnah* books and the travail of the *Shekhinah* in exile. And it was to Reb Zalman as if she herself was a personification of the teachings, a hidden light veiled from the world and unable to reveal herself to the people.

"Do you know, Reb Zalman," she said, "How great is the pain of the engorgement due to the untaught Torah that is in my being? How, like the milk from a mother's breast, it wants to flow out in blessing and light?"

Reb Zalman nodded and replied, "It is true. Torah needs the giving as well as the receiving, in order that it may be 'teaching like rain' as Moses spoke of it in his last song. So please, Hannah Rochel, will you share some of your Torah? Tell me, whom do you see as the seven holy guests in the *sukkah*? We men speak of Abraham, Isaac, Jacob, Joseph, Moses, Aaron, and David—but who are the retinue of the Holy *Shekhinah*?"

Hannah Rochel began to chant:

"This has not been revealed in fullness
except that Leah is the second
and Rachel is the last
for Gevurah and Malchut,
but the total of the seven
are not yet revealed to the world.
As you are the first to ever ask this—
a vessel open to receive—
then you are given to understand
that Miriam is the well of Grace (Hesed)
and Leah weeps for the wrath of severity.
Hannah is the Beauty-heart of the praying woman,
and Rebeccah is the victory of enduring,
while Sarah is the shining of Hod
and Tamar is the womb-man of YeHU-daH in Yesod
and Rachel our Mother Malkhut."

Then she spoke further to Reb Zalman, saying, "Tell me, do you know the mystery of the station of the High Priest, of the clothes he wore and the rituals he performed? He was the groomsman of the *Matronita*—the female side of God—and in that was his greatness. He ministered in the way of the woman, serving the food of the Holy One and keeping His House as the Divine Presence would have him do. In holiness and beauty he tended the fire and the sacred vessels, the golden pots and pans in the House of God."

Reb Zalman now replied, "The sages once said not to 'make much talk with the women,' and I understand now that they meant we should transcend gender. So we cannot really continue this conversation until you cease to see me as 'a man' and I cease to see you as 'a woman.' "

She agreed and said, "Since I am aware that I have in former lives been a man, and since no doubt you have lived before as a woman, let us both reach the balance of the Andro-gynos within ourselves, and converse as we might do between earth lives."

"But," said Reb Zalman, "does not the Mishnah teach that the Andro-gynos is a 'lesser person' and ought not to rise in our conversation?"

She replied in the chant of inner teachings. "Is it not taught in the Kabbalah, that when the primal vessels burst in the first moments of creation, the highest sparks fell the furthest? Thus, this lower level of the Andros-gynos is only until the *Mashiach* comes, since we cannot yet fully appreciate that perfection. But when we will be redeemed, this balance will be the center of our inner being, no matter what gender the body we wear. For then the split will be healed in us, as it will have been between Him and Her, when YH joins VH, for on that Day YHVH will be One, and One too will be the Name."

So he said to her, "Hear, O Hannah Rochel, YHVH our God is One..."

And she, in turn, says, "Hear, O Zalman, YHVH our God is One..."

And they both chanted *Echad* long and in harmony.

Then she said, "With you I can remove the veil of the physical world, to share with you the teaching of the menorah. Is it not written, 'The soul is the candle of God?' Every person is a menorah, for there are seven lights in the human face; two eyes, two ears, two nostrils, and a mouth. The menorah of women had to be hidden as mine was hidden all my life, or else the ignorant ones would have harmed the light. But since you said the *Echad* with me and put your *kavanah* to the One of the Ending, I feel free to let my menorah shine, for I trust that you will not harm it." And once again, she intoned the teaching chant:

> "The holy Apter taught:
> The anointing oil
> used to anoint the tent
> and the holy vessels
> in the sanctuary
> had the property
> to bring the tabernacle to life.

So I say that
the Menorah, too, was anointed
and it, too, came to life,
and when it was lit
the sanctuary awakened to awareness.

Soon will be the Feast of Hannukah,
and with the hempwool
in which the etrog was packed,
you will spin the wicks
and you will fill the lamp with oil
and light the wicks.
And we have been taught
that if one had no lamp base,
it could even be made from potatoes.
For you have learned about the wick—the body;
and you have learned about the oil—the soul;
and you have learned about the flame,
but you have not learned the secret of the Menorah.

For it is, NUR MAH,
the "light of forty-five"—
and what is forty-five? Mah?
It stands for ADAM...
Now tell me, Reb Zalman,
is ADAM male or female?
Is it not the number
of the Holy Name
as being the world of Atzilut—
YUD HA VAV HA—
and this is the MAH
which joins the NUR
and forms the MENORAH.

Now why do we choose
to have a silver Menorah
if we can?
Because the secret of the Menorah
is that She is Woman,

silver like the moon.

For the real miracle
why the lights burned
for eight days
is because of the Menorah,
for it was the Menorah herself
that stretched the oil
to burn for eight days."

Hannah Rochel then veiled her face again and prepared to leave, but even then, Reb Zalman saw only the menorah. He sat for what seemed like hours, contemplating the Menorah in all things, creating the vessel that contains the light. Over and over he kept repeating, "menorah, Mah Norah, Mah Nur..."

Before his eyes, the menorah turned to a fiery seraph, and that again to the letter ALEPH. He saw the image of the letter Yud on top and the Yud below, with the Vav on an angle, joining them together. Then the Aleph began to dance, and spun with both the Yuds in balance on either side, and he knew that the Aleph was Andro-gynos, the balance of Wholeness...and, alas, he also understood that we today are in a world that began with the BETH of twoness.

He had been given a glimpse of how the earth is ADAMAH—HAADAM, not forty-five, but fifty, and in his heart he thanked the Creator that the fifty gates of Understanding had been opened to Hannah Rochel. As the Sages said, "Extra Understanding was given to Woman more than Man." ISHAH—WOMAN = 306 and HA-MENORAH = 306, and he had been given a glimpse of that...

The two Feivels came over and roused Reb Zalman from his thoughts. Feivel the Dark handed him a note that Hannah Rochel had left before she departed. What it said was:

"All my life, people sought to change me, to stifle my Torah and extinguish my light. But what I have revealed to you cannot be hidden forever. You have received it in secret, but there will come a time when this Menorah will shine for all to see. As it is written in

the Holy Zohar in the story of Noah, when you see the rainbow shining in its fullest splendor, then will the Messiah come. The rainbow —a seven-rayed Menorah—will be the sign of the Holy Light."

Reb Zalman looked up and saw that the blizzard was over and the sky was clear. But before returning to Zholkiev, he took out his Hannukah menorah, some polishing powder—and began to weep. The tears mixed with the powder, and polished the menorah until it shone like the holy light in Hannah Rochel's eyes.

APPENDIX B

A fragment of a prayer note found in Reb Zalman's
Siddur, seemingly a preface to his *quittel* reading.

Oy holy God, sweet *Tattenyu.*
You gave me this task and I took it loving you.
You also showed me that I am a new thing unheard of
before—a rebbe who is not a zaddik!—not even an in-
betweener! but one whom Your justice counts among the
sinners and it is true. Oy!

You made me a deceiver. You did. So They come because
they think I have something to teach them when in truth all
I know I learn from them. What is my worth, God, when I
give them only what is theirs?!

They think that I bless them and when I *mammesh* steal
their blessings and then hand them to them as my gift?

And I tell you God! I can't say the blessing: "Thank you for not making me a woman." When you give me living Torah do I not go through labor? When I console and feed your flock am I not like a nursing mother? If not for their Torah what could the other Torah have taught me?

Then I see through the words to you that "They" say, "Thank You who has made me according to your will."

Would Dear God! *Halevay!* that you remake me according to your will.

Until then You must help me. You must at least, the very least answer my prayer on behalf of......
(A list of names follows.)

GLOSSARY

(All terms are Hebrew unless otherwise noted)

Adamah — Earth, Humus.

Adonai Elohenu, Adonai Ehad — "The Lord our God, the Lord is One." From the *Shema*.

Aggadah — the non-halachic material in the Talmud, primarily consisting of legends.

Aleph — The first letter of the Hebrew Alphabet.

aliyah — literally "to ascend." The term used for those who choose to live in Israel and also to denote the honor extended to a worshiper who ascends the *bimah* in the synagogue for the Torah-reading services.

'Alma d'Shikra — kabbalistic term for World of Illusion or World of Lies. It is often contrasted with *Olam ha Emeth*, the World of Truth.

Amidah — the prayers also known as *Shmoneh Esreh* or the Eighteen Benedictions, which are found in all daily, Sabbath, and holiday services. This prayer is recited while standing.

Arabot — the seventh and highest heaven.

Aron HaKodesh — literally "the holy Ark." The Ark of the Covenant, in which the *Sefer Torah* is kept.

Atzilut — Emanation, the highest realm of pure Divinity only attainable by Intuition.

Baal Tefillah — a Master of prayer.

bat kol — a heavenly voice.

Beit Din — a rabbinic court convened to decide issues relating to the Halakhah.

Beit Knesset — a house of prayer.

Beit Midrash — a house of study. Traditionally next to the *Beit Knesset*.

beshert — Yiddish for "predestined."

Beth — The second letter of the Hebrew Alphabet.

bris — literally "Covenant." The circumcision given to every male Jewish child on the eighth day after birth. The complete term is *bris milah*, or "Covenant of the Circumcision."

daven/davening — Yiddish for "to pray." Refers especially to the intense prayers of the Hasidim, who, following the dictum of the Baal Shem Tov, attempt to *daven* with *kavanah*, or spiritual intensity.

Drash — an interpretation of a passage of the Bible. Also the third level of *Pardes,* the system of interpretation of sacred texts, representing allegory.

d'var Torah — literally "word of Torah." A concise lesson in Torah, interpreting a passage in the Bible or Talmud or another sacred text.

Ehad — literally One.

Ein Sof — literally "endless" or "infinite." The highest, unknowable aspect of the Divinity.

erev — the eve of the Sabbath or a holy day, on which it begins.

Eretz Yisrael — the Land of Israel.

Eruv/Eruvin — *Eruvin,* one of the tractates of the Mishnah, deals with the laws concerning Sabbath restrictions and methods to remove difficulties relating to these laws by the creation of *Eruvin* (singular: *Eruv*) or boundaries.

Gabbai — overseer of synagogue procedure; a position of honor and trust.

Gan Eden — the Garden of Eden; also a term for the Earthly Paradise, in conjunction with the Celestial Paradise.

Gehenna — the Place where the souls of the wicked are punished and purified; the equivalent of Purgatory.

Gevurah — Might, Power, (the Sephirah — Divine attribute of) severity.

gilgul — the transmigration of souls. The kabbalistic equivalent of the belief in reincarnation.

HaAdam — The Man, Human.

Halevay — an exclamation of pleading used colloquially.

Hanukah — festival celebrated for eight days to commemorate the successful struggle of the Jews led by Judah Maccabee and the rededication of the Holy Temple in Jerusalem.

Hanukiah — the special menorah for Hanukah, which has eight candlesticks and a ninth for the *Shammash* (servant).

Hatavat Halom — a ritual in which a dream is interpreted.

Havdolah — literally "to distinguish" or "to separate." The ceremony performed at the end of the Sabbath, denoting the separation of the Sabbath from the rest of the week.

Hazan — a cantor.

Hesed — Grace, Loving-kindness, (the Sefirah — attribute of *Gedulah*) largesse.

Herra Kadisha — the society that fulfills all the ritual requirements for a Jewish funeral.

Huppah — the wedding canopy.

Hod — Glory, splendor (attribute of) elegance.

Hosha'na Rabbah — the seventh day of *Sukkos*.

Ishah — Woman.

Kadosh — literally, "Holy." Holiness, sacredness.

Kapparot — an ancient custom performed on the morning of the eve of *Yom Kippur* in which a fowl is taken and swung around the head while specified verses are recited.

kasha — (Yiddish from the Slavic) — cracked buckwheat cooked into a mushlike consistency and served with meat and in soup. Literally *"Kushya,"* "difficulty" in Aramaic.

kavanah — literally "intention." Spiritual intensity, especially in prayer. A common saying is "Prayer without *kavanah* is like a body without *neshamah* (soul)."

ketubah — a traditional marriage contract, written in Aramaic, which lists the groom's obligations to the bride.

Kotel — literally "wall." The Wailing Wall in Jerusalem.

Lamed-vav Tzaddikim — the thirty-six Just Men or Hidden Saints who, according to the tradition, exist in every generation, and for whom the world continues to exit.

L'Hayim — literally "to life." A common Jewish toast.

Maariv — the evening prayer service, recited after nightfall.

Maaseh — a tale or story, often a folktale.

Malach Hamoves — the Angel of Death.

Malkhut — Majesty, Kingdom, (the Sefirah of) the Divine Presence, the *Shekhinah.*

Mashiach — the Messiah.

Matronita — an alternative word for *Shekhinah* and *Malkhut*, Divine female aspect, the Queen-God.

matzos — unleavened bread baked for Passover to commemorate the Exodus from Egypt.

melamed — a teacher.

menorah — the seven-branched candelabrum described in the Bible and used in Temple days.

Merkavah — literally "chariot." The Merkavah is the divine chariot in the version of Ezekiel.

Mezzuzah — literally "doorpost." A small case containing a piece of parchment upon which is written the proclamation that begins "*Shema Yisrael.*" This case is affixed to the right doorpost of a Jew's home, in accordance with the biblical injunction.

mikveh — the ritual bath in which women immerse themselves after menstruation has ended. It is also used occasionally by men for purposes of ritual purification.

Minhah — the daily prayer service, which is recited after noon and before sunset.

minhag — a religious custom that has become generally accepted, at least within a community.

Minyan — the quorum of ten males over the age of thirteen that is required for any congregational service.

Misnagid — an opponent of the Hasidim.

mitzvah/mitzvot — a divine commandment. There are 613 *mitzvot* listed in the Torah. The term has also come to mean any good deed.

Mohel — a person trained to perform a circumcision.

Nahash Hakadmoni — the Primal Serpent, one manifestation of the Evil One, or Satan. Primarily a kabbalistic concept derived from the encounter of Eve and the serpent in Genesis.

Nehama — literally, "consolation." A commonly used Hebrew name.

neshamah — a soul.

nigun/nigunim — traditional chant to a prayer.

Olam Hatohu — the world of chaos. The world before the Creation.

parashah — one of the fifty-four sections of the Torah, which is read as the section of the week. *Parsheot* is plural. Used interchangeably with *Sidrah.*

Pardes — literally "orchard," and also a root term for "Paradise." Also an acronym of a system of textual exegesis, based on four levels of interpretation: *peshat* (literal), *remez* (symbolical), *drash* (allegorical) and *sod* (mystical).

Pargod — literally "curtain." In Jewish mysticism it refers to the curtain that is said to hang before the Throne of Glory.

Pesach — the Jewish holiday of Passover, commemorating the exodus from Egypt.

Peshat — the literal kind of textual exegesis. Also the first level of biblical interpretation in the system known as Pardes.

qlaf — a small piece of parchment on which the text of a *Mezzuzah* or amulet is written.

qvittel — a note written by a petitioner to a Hasidic rabbi, explaining why an audience with the rabbi has been requested.

remez — literally "a hint." The second level of interpretation in the system known by the acronym *Pardes.* It implies the perception that the meaning has moved from the literal to the symbolic level.

Ribbono Shel Olam — literally "Master of the World" or "Master of the Universe." A name used to address God.

Rosh Hashanah — the Jewish New Year, which takes place on the first day of Tishri. Tradition says that the world was created on Rosh Hashanah.

Rosh Hodesh — literally, "the head of the month." The day of the new moon, which is observed as a holy day and festival.

Rosh Yeshivah — the head of a *Yeshivah.*

Seder — the traditional Passover ceremonial meal, during which the Haggadah describing the deliverance from Egypt is recited.

Sefer Torah — the scroll of the Torah.

Sefirot — emanations, ten in all, through which the world came into existence, according to kabbalistic theory.

Sha'ar Hakedusha — literally "Gate of Holiness." A text written in the 16th century in Safed by Hayim Vital.

Shabbas Shira — the Sabbath on which the portion of the Bible concerning the singing of the Song at the Sea is read.

Shabbas — the Sabbath.

Shahareis — the morning prayers.

Shalom — literally "peace." Also a greeting and salutation.

Shalom Aleichem — literally "Peace be with you."

shammash — literally "servant." The beadle of a synagogue.

Sheheheyanu — a blessing recited over a fruit tasted for the first time that year and on other occasions, such as when putting on a new garment for the first time or moving into a new house.

Shekhinah — literally "to dwell." The Divine Presence, usually identified as a feminine aspect of the Divinity. Also identified as the Bride of God and the Sabbath Queen.

Shema — the central prayer of Judaism: *Shema Yisrael, Adonai Elohanu, Adonai Ahad* — Hear O Israel, the Lord our God, the Lord is One. Based on Deut. 6:4-9.

Shema Yisrael — the first two words of the central prayer in Judaism: Hear, O Israel.

shidduch — a match made between two people which leads to matrimony.

shofar — a ram's horn trumpet used by the ancient Hebrews in battle. It is sounded as part of some high religious observances.

Shulhan Aruch — the Code of Jewish Law compiled by Joseph Karo in the 16th century which is the most widely used.

shtetl (Yiddish) — a small rural village inhabited almost exclusively by Jews.

Siddur — prayer book.

Simhas Torah — the concluding day of the festival of *Sukkos* on which the cycle of reading from the Torah is concluded and begun again.

Sod — the fourth, mystical level of the four-level system of interpretation represented by the acronym *Pardes*.

sopher — a scribe, whose duties include copying and repairing the *Sefer Torah,* and, among the Hasidim, recording the teachings of their rebbes. A famous scribe is Rabbi Nathan of Nemerov, scribe of Rabbi Nachman of Bratslav.

Sopher's Tikkun — a very precise text that serves the scribe as a model.

Sukkah — a booth in which Jews were commanded to live for seven days so as to remember the Israelites who resided in booths during their exodus from Egypt. Its roof must be covered with boughs, through which the stars are visible and which are not attached.

Sukkos — a seven day festival beginning on the 15th of Tishri, during which all meals are eaten in a *Sukkah*.

tallis/tallisim — a four cornered prayer shawl with fringes at the corners, worn by men during the morning prayer services.

Tanach — an acronym for the Bible.

Tattenyu — diminutive for father.

tefillin — phylacteries worn at the morning services (except on the Sabbath) by men and boys over the age of thirteen.

tekhelet — a blue dye, long considered lost, which Jews were enjoined to color a thread in the fringes of the *tallis*.

teshuvah — repentence.

tikkun — restoration and redemption.

tsitsis — the fringes of the *tallis*.

Tu-bishevat — the 15th of Shevat, known as the New Year for Trees, on which it is customary to plant saplings in Israel. It is also the day on which almond blossoms are said to first appear.

tzaddik/tzaddikim — an unusually righteous and spiritually pure person. Hasidim believe their rebbes to be *tzaddikim*.

tzedekah — charity.

Viduy — a confession addressed directly to God for the purpose of repentence.

yahrtzeit — Yiddish term meaning the anniversary of the death of a close relative.

yeshivah — Jewish traditional school devoted primarily to the study of the Talmud and rabbinic literature.

Yesod — Foundation (attribute of) fecundity.

Yetzer Hara — the Evil Inclination.

Yiddiskite/Yiddish — a sense of Jewishness or association with Jewish traditions.

Yom Kippur — the most solemn day of the Jewish religious year, spent in fasting and prayer.

Zaida — Yiddish grandfather.

Rabbi Zalman Schachter-Shalomi has been at the forefront of a pioneering renewal of Jewish spirituality in the contemporary world. A modern master of the methods of transformational psychology, he uses prayer and meditation, movement and song, storytelling and philosophical discourse, to present the central teachings of Hasidism and Kabbalah along with other universal spiritual truths gleaned from Sufi, Buddhist, Shamanic, Native American and traditional religious sources. Born in Poland in 1924 and raised in Vienna, he was ordained as a rabbi at the Lubavitch Yeshivah in Brooklyn, and has a doctorate from Hebrew Union College. He has served as a congregational rabbi, a Hillel rabbi, a Hebrew school principal, and as the head of *P'nai Or*, a religious fellowship. He has also taught religious studies at the University of Manitoba, where he was head of the Department of Near Eastern and Judaic Studies, and Temple University. His books include *Fragments of a Future Scroll, The First Step,* and *Sparks of Light.* Reb Zalman currently works with students through his "Wisdom School," a dynamic example of the path of the heart, turning seminars into magic, magic into mystery and mystery into the illumination of our hearts and minds.

Howard Schwartz was born in St. Louis in 1945, and teaches at the University of Missouri-St. Louis. He is the author of two books of poems, *Vessels* and *Gathering the Sparks*, and of several books of fiction, including *The Captive Soul of the Messiah* and *Rooms of the Soul*. He has edited the anthologies *Imperial Messages, Voices within the Ark*, and *Gates to the New City*, and three volumes of Jewish folktales, *Elijah's Violin, Miriam's Tambourine*, and *Lilith's Cave*. He is currently editing a collection of Jewish mystical tales.

Yitzhak Greenfield was born in Brooklyn in 1932 and immigrated to Israel in 1951. He currently lives in Ein Kerem outside of Jerusalem. His paintings, collages and prints have been exhibited in numerous one-man shows and are in the collections of many museums including The Metropolitan Museum of Modern Art, The Jewish Museum, The Brooklyn Museum, the Magnes Museum in Berkeley, Victoria and Albert Museum, London, Bibliotheque Nationale, Paris, The Israel Museum in Jerusalem and the Tel Aviv Museum. He has previously illustrated the book, *Gathering the Sparks*, by Howard Schwartz.

Dear Reader of *The Dream Assembly*,

If you have enjoyed Reb Zalman's stories in the Hassidic tradition, you may be interested in related literature and recordings from Gateways Books & Tapes. Our offerings cover a wide range from metaphysics, shamanism, and transformational psychology to metaphysical humor, fine art, contemporary music, spoken word audio and experimental video.

For a current book and tape catalog, or to contact Zalman Schachter-Shalomi and Howard Schwartz regarding their work, lectures, workshops and other resources related to contemporary Judaism and Kabbalah, write to Gateways at the address shown below. You may also phone Gateways for information on study programs and other resources that we offer.

Gateways Books and Tapes
PO Box 370
Nevada City, CA 95959
Tel. (916) 477-1116; Fax (916) 265-4321